The Angel Babies

.X.

DomE

The Angel Babies

.X.

DomE

Clive Alando Taylor

authorHOUSE

AuthorHouse™ UK
1663 Liberty Drive
Bloomington, IN 47403 USA
www.authorhouse.co.uk
Phone: 0800.197.4150

Published by AuthorHouse 11/25/2016

ISBN: 978-1-5246-6661-3 (sc)
ISBN: 978-1-5246-6660-6 (e)

Print information available on the last page.

This book is printed on acid-free paper.

Angelus Domini

INSPIRIT* ASPIRE* ESPRIT* INSPIRE*

Inspiration is one thing and genius is another,
but I now know that I owe all the art of my heart
to the one perfect love form of my God.
A form that is without blemish,
As it is only to this understanding
that I do yield and surrender
but never giving up on hope or freedom
Not now not ever.

Angelus Domini

D O M E .X.

INSPIRIT* ASPIRE* ESPRIT* INSPIRE*

Because of the things that have first become proclaimed within the spirit, and then translated in the soul, in order for the body to then become alive and responsive or to aspire, or to be inspired, if only then for the body to become a vessel, or a catalyst, or indeed an instrument of will, with which first the living spirit that gave life to it, along with the merits and the meaning of life, and the instruction and the interpretation of life, is simply to understand that the relationship between the spirit and the soul, are also the one living embodiment with which all things are one, and become connected and interwoven by creating, or causing what we can come to call, or refer to as the essence, or the cradle, or the fabric of life, which is in itself part physical and part spirit.

And so it is, that we are all brought in being, along with this primordial and spiritual birth, and along with this the presence or the origins of the spirit, which is also the fabric and the nurturer of the soul with which the body can be formed, albeit that by human standards, this act of nature however natural, can now take place through the act of procreation or consummation, and so it is with regard to this living spirit that we are also upon our natural and physical birth, given a name and a number, inasmuch that we represent, or become identified by a color, or upon our created formation and distinction of identity, we become recognized by our individuality.

But concerning the Angels, it has always been of an interest to me how their very conception, or existence, or origin from nature and imagination, could have become formed and brought into being, as overtime I have heard several stories of how with the event of the first creation of man, that upon this event, that all the Angels were made to accept and to serve in God's creation of man, and that man was permitted to give command to these Angels in the event of his life, and the trials of his life which were to be mastered, but within this godly decree and narrative, we also see that there was all but one Angel that either disagreed or disapproved with, not only the creation of man, but also with the formation of this covenant between God and man, and that all but one Angel was Satan, who was somewhat displeased with God's creation of man, and in by doing so would not succumb or show respect or demonstrate servility or humility toward man or mankind.

As overtime it was also revealed to me, that with the creation of the Angels, that it was also much to their advantage as it was to ours, for the Angels themselves to adhere to this role and to serve in the best interest of man's endeavors upon the face of the earth, as long as man himself could demonstrate and become of a will and a nature to practice his faith with a spirit, and a soul, and a body that would become attuned to a godly or godlike nature, and in by doing so, and in by believing so, that all of his needs would be met with accordingly.

And so this perspective brings me to question my own faith and ideas about the concept and the ideology of Angels, insomuch so that I needed to address and to explore my own minds revelation, and to investigate that which I was told or at least that which I thought I knew concerning the Angels along with the juxtaposition that if

Satan along with those Angels opposed to serving God's creation of man, and of those that did indeed seek to serve and to favor God's creation and to meet with the merits, and the dreams, and the aspirations of man, that could indeed cause us all to be at the mercy and the subjection of an externally influential and internal spiritual struggle or spiritual warfare, not only with ourselves, but also with our primordial and spiritual identity.

And also because of our own conceptual reasoning and comprehension beyond this event, is that we almost find ourselves astonished into believing that this idea of rights over our mortal souls or being, must have begun or started long ago, or at least long before any of us were even souls inhabiting our physical bodies here as a living presence upon the face of the earth, and such is this constructed dilemma behind our beliefs or identities, or the fact that the names, or the numbers that we have all been given, or that have at least become assigned to us, is simply because of the fact that we have all been born into the physical world.

As even I in my attempts, to try to come to terms with the very idea of how nature and creation could allow so many of us to question this reason of totality, if only for me to present to you the story of the Angel Babies, if only to understand, or to restore if your faith along with mine, back into the realms of mankind and humanity, as I have also come to reflect in my own approach and understanding of this narrative between God and Satan and the Angels, that also in recognizing that they all have the power to influence and to subject us to, as well as to direct mankind and humanity, either to our best or worst possibilities, if only then to challenge our primordial spiritual origin within the confines of our own lifestyles, and practices and beliefs, as if in our own efforts and practices that we are all each and every one of us, in subjection or at least examples and products of both good and bad influences.

Which is also why that in our spiritual nature, that we often call out to these heavenly and external Angelic forces to approach us, and to heal us, and to bless us spiritually, which is, or has to be made to become a necessity, especially when there is a humane need for us to call out for the assistance, and the welfare, and the benefit of our own souls, and our own bodies to be aided or administered too, or indeed for the proper gifts to be bestowed upon us, to empower us in such a way, that we can receive guidance and make affirmations through the proper will and conduct of a satisfactory lesson learnt albeit through this practical application and understanding, if only to attain spiritual and fruitful lives.

As it is simply by recognizing that we are, or at some point or another in our lives, have always somewhat been open, or subject to the interpretations of spiritual warfare by reason of definition, in that Satan's interpretation of creation is something somewhat of contempt, in that God should do away with, or even destroy creation, but as much as Satan can only prove to tempt, or to provoke God into this reckoning, it is only simply by inadvertently influencing the concepts, or the ideologies of man, that of which whom God has also created to be creators, that man through his trials of life could also be deemed to be seen in Satan's view, that somehow God had failed in this act of creation, and that Satan who is also just an Angel, could somehow convince God of ending creation, as Satan himself cannot, nor does not possess the power to stop or to end creation, which of course is only in the hands of the creator.

And so this brings me back to the Angels, and of those that are in favor of either serving, or saving mankind from his own end and destruction, albeit that we are caught up in a primordial spiritual fight, that we are all engaged in, or by reason of definition born into, and so it is only by our choices that we ultimately pay for our sacrifice, or believe in our rights to life, inasmuch that we are all lifted up to our greatest effort or design, if we can learn to demonstrate and to accept our humanity in a way that regards and reflects our greater desire or need, to be something more than what we choose to believe is only in the hands of God the creator or indeed a spirit in the sky.

It was very much my intention not to state the name of any particular place in the script as I thought that the telling of the story of the Angel Babies is in itself about believing in who you are, and also about facing up to your fears. The Angel Babies is also set loosely in accordance with the foretelling of the Bibles Revelations.

I thought it would be best to take this approach, as the writing of the script is also about the Who, What, Where, When, How and Why scenario that we all often deal with in our ongoing existence. It would also not be fair to myself or to anyone else who has read the Angel Babies to not acknowledge this line of questioning, for instance, who are we? What are we doing here? Where did we come from? And when will our true purpose be known? And how do we fulfil our true potential to better ourselves and others, the point of which are the statements that I am also making in the Angel Babies and about Angels in particular,

Is that if we reach far into our minds we still wonder, where did the Angels come from and what is their place in this world. I know sometimes that we all wish and pray for the miracle of life to reveal itself but the answer to this mystery truly lives within us and around us, I only hope that you will find the Angel Babies an interesting narrative and exciting story as I have had in bringing it to life, after all there could be an Angel Baby being born right now.

After these things I looked and behold a door standing open in Heaven and the first voice which I heard was like a (Trumpet!) speaking with me saying come up here and I will show you things which must take place after this.

Immediately I was in the spirit and behold a throne set in Heaven and one sat on the throne and he who sat there was like a Jasper and a Sardius Stone in appearance, And there was a Rainbow around, In appearance like an Emerald.

Time is neither here or there, it is a time in between time as it is the beginning and yet the end of time. This is a story of the Alpha and the Omega, the first and the last and yet as we enter into this revelation, we begin to witness the birth of the Angel Babies a time of heavenly conception when dying Angels gave birth to Angelic children who were born to represent the order of the new world. The names of these Angel Babies remained unknown but they carried the Seal of their fathers written on their foreheads, and in all it totaled one hundred and forty four thousand Angels and this is the story of one of them.

D O M E . X .

Now the descendents of the Angel Babies is hereby as follows, as it is hereby duly recorded as Haven of Simeon, and Stefan of Hark, Angelo of Stefan, and Nephi and Ruen of Ophlyn who are also the offspring of the consummate forbearers of the Earth Angels which are hereby as follows, for they are Selah, and Mercidiah, and Kali Ma and Josephine and Anahita and Leoine.

As for the recollections of these Angels of the Empyreans, we had by now entered into a time when the World was out of step and disconnected from the original beliefs that had once influenced the order of everyday life, and so it was that those who were amongst the Earth Angels would be challenged and to take the reins of humanity toward their new equilibrium, if only to uproot the cancerous seeds of their constructions, and to lead the people of the Dome back towards their freedom, in seeking out, and to undo what Mankind had done to the World, and yet it could only be pronounced, and put upon the head of the Blackest if not the Darkest of all Angels of the Empyreans, and yet the only one Angel found worthy to be given such a task as this, and who else of course but none other than the Angel of indifference, Angel Ruen the Son of Ophlyn the Herald Angel, of whose own personal redemption could only be successfully won over and granted, if he were to serve by dismantling this Dome of ungodly construction, in order to gain back his honor in favor of the Empyreans.

As it was also that these newly implemented belief systems, that were of a diminished nature, due to the reality that life

9

had by now become less meaningful, and almost to the point of extinction, and so within this new automated and technological world, surrogates and avatars and cloning were permitted on a mass scale to reinforce the population of Mankind, as for this mass calling of this reproduction which was deemed necessary for regulating its workforce, as even some of the elders of this new Dome, who were still wholly human but very much corrupted by this new order, would also be caused to change the course of evolution and the destiny of humanity through their cloning programs and other practices, such as scientifically transmitting their own personal DNA codes into the Human Genealogy Pool, through a program called Genetic X, so as to reproductively create the perfect species in their own form, which was by now to be carried out globally, in order to select or deselect what time and place, and what type of being would be needed for any and every collaborative effort of usage at any time for the universal workforce or any other intended role, as these were called the Generations, and yet each being that was cloned or created, could only be needed or enhanced for that one singular purpose, so as to be employed in any representative House in having its membership based upon its' universal skills of functions and uses.

Now it was that during Angel Ruen's flight of descent and disengagement from the outer realms where Angel Haven had once given over to his debatable friend and Ally, the influences of his instructions over to the aspectual awareness's of Angel Ruen's discontented if not restless heart, that during his flight of departure of going out and seeking the one known as Obadiah 144, who was perhaps the only Elder of the Dome left, who still practiced the faith of the old and original ways, albeit behind closed doors and under the guise of acting as a Moderator of the 12 Houses, that it was upon his fight of descent, that the somewhat harshly utterances of Angel Ruen resounded woefully throughout the heavens, if only in realizing that Man had been at war with himself since the beginning of time, and even now had sought to cut the umbilical cord that ties the birth of the Earth to Heavens.

As Man in his attempt to master his environment, is now found to be constructing fortresses and creating false God's in his doctrine, if only to worship in the name of such abhorrence and godforsaken practices, of that with which is not his to acquire, and that which is beyond his grasp, as never before in the history of the world, has such an unprecedented influence impacted itself upon the face of humanity, except that Man had drafted and written and rewritten his own history, of that with which we have in turn had to fulfill in his stead, if not by himself, then by the exceptions of the Angels of the Empyreans, and the Angels of the Celestial Abode, if only for us to serve as a reminder of the sacrifices of that which we have made before God, as Man has set himself above and beyond all things knowingly destroying nature and questionably arguing amongst themselves to bring about the downfall of Humanity, in ignorantly believing he is above all things, and yet man is the problem as well as the solution to this mayhem, and yet the Spirit of man is permitted to wonder upon even encroaching upon the laws of the Heavens that has permitted him to exist, and so how shall it be if I am to swing my blade in the name of Yahweh Elohim, if only to bring forth the noble truths that divide Man from Men, when he himself is amongst the divided of the his divisive and erroneous ways and methods.

And so it was, that of all the human traits that were constantly being reproduced for production due to the ageing defects of cell degeneration, and yet for some miraculous purpose it was found to be that at this time, that a child had naturally been conceived, somewhere in Dome Europe, albeit that the parents of this newborn infant had met, and come from different parts of the Dome international, as it had come about through the exchanges of two completely different and separate generations, and through their membership as young students of being of the same House, that had served in bringing about this miracle however unintended, and so it was that to save Humanity from Mankind's path of destruction and desecration, that an intervention was made by the Angels of the Empyreans, that these two separate Houses, that one of the elders known as Obadiah 144, who would be permitted to maintain the secrecy of this act, in that humanity might be saved, as it was unbeknown to the young father of this infant child, Joseph Blake, that such a thing had even transpired and taken place through him, and through this short time of period with which he had spent with Mary Hampden, a student with whom he had met upon a student exchange program that was constructed to introduce and to integrate the potential hopefuls of their allied Households to be introduced for the future of the Domes, as it was during the course of his initiation into the Household of the 7th Generations, that Joseph Blake was treated somewhat differently from the others by his social peers group, in that they amused themselves around him, and treated him more like an outsider because of his naïve and innocent nature.

The date is Wednesday 31st December 2999 New Years Eve, and somewhere in the Precinct of a City of a prominent building

registered as Stereotypical, is where we find Obadiah 144 making a recording of one of his many prophetic statements concerning the progress of the current times.

Obadiah 144

Now as it was prophesied long ago that the world would change so much so, that it would become unrecognizable beyond itself, and would be referred to at this time as the Dome, and so it was that the future governance of the Dome which would consist of independent houses of regulations, along with separate departments of equal measure, created to meet with, and to address the demands, and the needs placed upon the people as well as the infrastructure and implementation of Governmental policy, outsourced to independent bodies and organizations including subversive elects unaccountable to anyone in divided bureaucratic departments., discarding the knowledge and the philosophical idea that the teachings of God now declared discarded and somewhat redundant, as we are living in an age where Heaven had cease to move above and beyond the Earth, which some would say in itself was the beginning of this unpredictable age, as I Obadiah 144 am also aware and present of this unique time, in giving rise to this waking testament, so as to submit in prayer, in realizing that the Ophanim upon the Throne of God had interactively ceased to account for the many vast and varied multitudes of Humanity, now found to be decreasing in their many population, although it could not have been foreseen as to what consequential irreversible actions would have impacted upon the inhabitants of these most densely and populated Cities now referred to as Domes.

Meanwhile Joseph Blake is in a local shop purchasing a few basic groceries.

Joe

Can I have a packet of menthol cigarettes, a pint of milk, some coffee and sugar please?

Assistant

Is that it?

Joe

Yeah, that's it thank you

Assistant

How do you wanna pay?

Joe

Can I pay by credit on my chip, although I think it's' been playin up a bit

Assistant

You should try by rubbing a silver coin on the palm of your hand that normally triggers the circuits

14

Joe

Silver coins, I never thought of that, thanks, I'm just not quite sure how much credit I've got remaining, as I've been on a spending spree on a trip I took, yuh know student exchange and all that

Assistant

That's ok, thanks for shopping with us, please call again

Joe

Yeah thanks, ok, bye

....

Upon his arrival back to his place of residence, Joseph Blake receives a message from a newly acquainted friend Christian Scott, as he is relaxing within his student accommodation somewhere in the University Dome Complex.

Chris

Beep Beep …Joseph Blake…You've got mail…Beep Beep

Hi Joseph, its' me Christina, I've been trying to call you on your video phone, but I didn't get an answer, anyway I sent you a photo message about tonight and I've decided to meet up with Seth so that we can head down to that new eighty four room complex in the Precinct, I think it's' called Stereotypical, anyway I'm just calling to see if you still wanna come with us or meet us there, ya know, so that we can see the New Year together and have some fun at the same time, anyway it starts at Nine o clock and goes on until dawn, so give me a call or send me a text or something, and we'll meet you there, ok bye for now Joe, ps Taurus rules byeeee!

....

Later on that day Joseph Blake who is a first year initiate student of the University household of Generation 7, is at home relaxing and interactively working on his computer, which unbeknown to him is also being hacked by an operative who goes by the codename of Agent Rumsfold who is part of a Dark Net Government organisation that tracks and monitors new initiates as of when they are implanted with their newly assigned Digital Chip that records all their usage and data placed beneath their skin or upon their personal being.

Joe

Computer, Access 1.4.7, Joseph Blake Diary, …Logging On
Dear diary its' been a hard week but I got loads of work done and I'm now preparing for the winter holidays, as its' been a challenging first year so far with some tough assignments but I manage to get through all of it without doing to badly, oh yeah I made a couple of new friends, some people I'm still getting to know but there's a girl, her name is Christina and she's really beautiful and quite amazing but the thing is she's got some really weird friends, one of them is this guy called Seth, well they call him 'Seth the Jester coz he gets up to all sorts of pranks, well he gets on my nerves, attempting or trying to be clever and an extrovert but Chris like him so I guess I have to make allowances, well to change the subject I haven't been feeling to good lately what with my condition and losing Mary last summer when I got back from Dome Europe, can't remember but to top that off I'm running out of credit, can't even do a week's shopping until I get some work to top up my points, or its' gonna be

cheese and bread sandwiches again' that's all I got left over, anyway I still need to decide whether I'm going to that new complex Chris invited me too, but no doubt if I don't go they'll only be on my case next semester, so I'll catch you later…Logging Off…Logging Off…

Agent Rumsfold

…Logging Off…Logging On…Beep…Digital Angel activated, initiating radio frequency transmission, stabilizing…overriding 3 digit access code, One…6… (1) Four…6… (4) Seven…6... (7) affirmative, programme active and complete…Logging Off…Good, now let's gets this mobile unit out of here before were detected, I wanna see for myself if the Black Angel can turn this kid away from becoming a potential graduate member of Generation 7, this so called God concept of Obadiah 144, has gone too far too soon, now Tork let's go, as the next stop is Stereotypical.

....

Obadiah 144

As it was also prophesied that all citizens of each country would be implanted with a digital chip in order to gain access to credit in order to use all amenities and to buy food and for the use of all services allocated and provided by their level of contribution to the state, as this also affected travel and the usage of all governmental facilities, which was held on a database of record of all its' citizens, which by now on the underground, was refereed to and called the mark of the beast.

Meanwhile Sethaniel Newton and Christina Scott, who are two second and third year students from 2 separate Houses are on

the phone talking to one another about meeting up to attend a University function that happens once a year to elect and select new representatives that compete to become new leaders overall for the 12 houses as a whole over the term of a one year period.

Seth

Is Joe coming tonight?

Chris

Yeah he's coming

Seth

Are you sure, when did you speak to him?

Chris

I called him earlier and I left a couple of messages, he's definitely coming, trust me, why?

Seth

No reason, just asking

Chris

Yeah right, I know you Seth, what you thinking?

Seth

No nothing seriously, I was just wondering if you told him what stereotypical was all about

Chris

Well I filled him in a bit, why is there something I should know?

Seth

No don't worry about it will be good, I don't wanna spoil it for you, well I hope he's coming, you know he doesn't go out much, I guess he's just adjusting to everything, ya know it being his first year and everything

Chris

That's right, so don't corrupt him Seth

Seth

I won't, I just wanna seduce him, ya know, well eventually anyway

Chris

You're kidding right Seth

Seth

No I'm serious, I think he's gorgeous don't you

Chris

But he's not your type

Seth

How do you know what he's like, I bet you he's a virgin, I bet you
he's never had sex in his entire life

Chris

So why do you have to be the first?

Seth

Well why do you?

Chris

Stop playing and give me a break

Seth

Because I do

Chris

You've got one dirty, filthy mind Seth, anyway I bet you he's straight

Seth

Oh I see it now, you just want pretty boy Floyd all for yourself, why don't we both shag him just for kicks

Chris

No! No way Seth, you're kidding, that's disgusting

Seth

We can take it in turns, you can shag him first and then I'll seduce him later, what do you reckon Chris, are you up for it?

Chris

Whatever you decide to do Seth is your own making, just don't get me involved into your perverted fantasies

Seth

Your such a pretentious little girl, what perversions, maybe I'm more adventurous but compared to you, well madam please

Chris

Just listen to yourself, who the hell do you think you are, you've just always gotta have it, don't you Seth, admit it

Seth

Yeah that's right and why not, I'll have you know that young minds are so easily persuaded

Christina Scott and Sethaniel Newton now arrive at the event called Stereotypical, and are about to enter the premises, which also requires an identification clarification to be made.

Chris

C'mon it's time to go in, anyway Seth I'll be surprised if he is

Seth

Yeah, well I'll be surprised if he even turns up

Chris

What you like, you and your gender bender friends?

Seth

Now you're taking the piss Chris, go on, go in and don't forget to access only levels 1 to 11, apparently the 12 houses have got some special reservation's going on tonight what with these celebrations and fake celebrities.

Chris

How do you know?

Seth

I know everything, now go in for Christ sakes

[SPEAK TO CONFIRM VOICE PROFILE]

Chris

Hi my name is Christina Scott, I'm 18 years old and I come from Dome Europe UK, and I am in my 2nd year degree course at University Dome Complex, studying, humanities, literary studies and philosophy. I can be quite cold and calculating but in a positive way and I am also very divisive and conservative in view, as well as stunning, attractive and did I say beautiful, of course, anyway I am a Taurean in case you didn't guess which means my feet are actually fixed firmly on the ground and being an earthly sign makes me practical and stable in every sense of the word. I owe all my femininity to Venus and I can be quite stubborn if I don't get my own way. My favourite colours are blue, orange, and yellow. Characteristically, I can be very determined and persistent. I am also very careful and cautious especially when it comes to men, and I am very productive, loving and affectionate. I love art, beauty and nature but I must say that I can forgive but never forget. I take my time to learn things almost surely, slowly and steadily and in the future I want to be a role model for strong professional, independent women, you know, the type who like to take the bull by the horns so to speak, well anyway its' a man's world but not anymore guys, so eat ya hearts out.

NOW PLACE HAND ON SCREEN AND KEY IN DIGITAL ANGEL CHIP CLASSIFICATION NUMBER]

Chris

CHRISTINA SCOTT – D.O.B – 21ST MAY 2981.NO.126

[SELECT LEVELS 1-12 AND DELETE AS APPROPRIATE]

Chris

Levels 1 to 11
[ACCESS ACKNOWLEDGE YOU MAY
ENTER LEVELS 1-11, ENJOY]

[SPEAK TO CONFIRM VOICE PROFILE]

Seth

Hi my name is Sethaniel Newton, I am 19 years old and I attend Dome Europe UK, I was born on the 21st of March so that makes me an Aries. I would best describe myself as being passionate, dynamic, and courageous with drive and initiative. I can also be impulsive, aggressive and dominating, I always follow my passion, which allows me to have a positive outlook and gives me a happy and exciting life. I like to explore a lot and I am always looking for adventure or the next best thing. I think my friends find me quite inspirational; they get a buzz out of my energy, which can be executed with great enthusiasm, currently I am an undergraduate about to complete my 3rd and final year studying multimedia, performing arts and sound recording technology. I like to be creative as well as expressive. I am a thinker with headstrong ideas and I never take any flak or bullshit from anyone, and although I am a bit of a joker I can be very direct and assertive as a person. I think I did exceptionally well in my previous exams, I am still waiting for the mid-term results, but I think I will pass with flying colours, who knows maybe a 1st or maybe a 1, 2. I think in the future I would like to become a professional singer songwriter or an artist and performer. I am really attracted to the glamour of the bright lights so I think I would like to invent a new sound although in this day and age nothing is new, maybe different but that seems to be the way of the world, buy life is what you make it and I love it and everything about it and everything in it

[NOW PLACE HAND OVER SCREEN AND KEY IN DIGITAL ANGEL CHIP CLASSIFICATION NUMBER]

Seth

SETHANIEL NEWTON – D.O.B – 20TH APRIL 2980.NO.217

[SELECT LEVELS 1 – 12 AND DELETE AS APPROPRITATE]

Seth

Levels 1 to 12

[ACCESS ACKNOWLEDGE YOU MAY ENTER LEVELS 1-12]

[ENJOY]

....

Obadiah 144

It was prophesied that the world would come to an end, and so it did, as the world at this time was by now known as the Dome, as it was at this time that due to the effects of global warming, that some parts of the Dome was less that inhabitable to support life in such a natural way as the previous centuries that had gone by, and so as the years that had preceded, the world as we knew it, was by now only a distant memory, that in finding that God would destroy the world in the last days was by now becoming a reality that the end was nigh, albeit with the exception that the Angels would descend to save and to salvage all that dwelt upon the Dome of that which they could, but as the Earth was no longer fit or completely sustainable to support all life in certain places of the globe, then what else would inevitably take place to save creation.

....

Upon their successful security admission into the venue known as Stereotypical, Christina and Sethaniel began to wander around and marvel as this spectacularly grand environment, as other students were also making their way through the high level security entrances, so as to be accepted into Stereotypical, which was said to be one of the most popular and significant eventful place for those amongst the Dome community to attend and make an appearance.

Chris

Look at those girls over there, they look like right tarts, look at what they're wearing, they've hardly got anything on, imagine coming out looking like that, they might as well have come naked

Seth

Your just jealous coz they look better than you do

Chris

Piss off Seth, I wouldn't be caught dead in that get up, they look like cheap little floozy's

Seth

What's the matter with you, you think you're so bloody special, your taking the piss because you never thought of wearing something as daring as that yourself, now leave it alone

Chris

Piss off Seth

Seth

Yeah right, jus coz your egos more inflated than a pregnant cow, you look like dolly the sheep

Chris

Don't say that, do I?

Seth

No I'm just kidding, darling please don't take me so seriously

Chris

That's not nice, your being spiteful

Seth

Ok sorry, I didn't mean it, but you do go on a bit Chris, why did I hurt your feelings?

Chris

You always say nasty things to me, say something nice for a change

Seth

Look Chris, I didn't create this madness, I'm just part of it just like you, if you can't take a joke then what's the point of coming out

Chris

Yeah I know, its' just that I don't want to be compared to a pregnant cow or a cloned sheep, I mean surely I'm worth much more than that, they think that cloning is better than natural conception or procreation, I can only wonder what it was like before the Generations got in

Seth

Do you mean to tell me that you prefer to be conceived using natural conception instead of cloning, are you mad, what are you saying girl

Chris

I'm saying that…I'm saying…oh forget it, I don' know what I'm saying but why did the governments develop an ideology to create a perfect race of people, if that was meant to be us, then its' completely and utterly ridiculous, look, at us, look what we've become, just because you're happy with everything Seth doesn't mean everyone else is alright about it

Seth

You better wake up Chris and stop dreaming, you know what's going on since science excelled in bio-technology everything is modified to suit its' intended environment, most of these companies are run by the Generations and there's no going back

Chris

Bio-technology, Science, what the hell are you talking about Seth, you sound like a flipping computer

Seth

What's the point of talking to you, you're a flipping clone, don't you get it, and clones are us! Genetic X and all that stuff

Christina begins to frown and then laugh with Sethaniel.

Chris

Yeah I get it, but I don't like it Seth

Seth

We are, what we are Chris, its' an improvement, otherwise we'd be corpses by now, what with all this gene pollution, and cross pollinated, and sterile fertilised embryos, did you know that more and more insects are completely resistant to insecticides, so that natural species all over the Dome are being destroyed even as we speak, new bacteria and viruses are spreading as a direct result and link through contact transference from plant to animal and from animal to human, and now were consuming more rodents and intersect in our legitimized food chain, made legal by the Governments of Dome, even before they finished testing it on God knows what, face it Chris, its' Biotechnology versus the natural environment, well what's left of it anyway, maybe I should compose a song or produce a film about it, do you think they will let me, yuh know tell the truth

Chris

Well modified Biological engineering and technology won by the looks of it, so I don't know what you'd sing or write about

Seth

Everyone of us are more equal now than we've ever been in the history of man

Chris

Bullshit, I don't' believe that

Seth

Believe what you want, but I know that you still have to accept it, and if you don't come to terms with it, it could affect your place and position in the 12 Houses, so don't be such a pessimist, there's always a positive side to life, who knows maybe our children will benefit from this and build a better future for themselves, don't you think?

Chris

Well one can always speculate with the idea of hope but I do think
your right, I mean after all, once we were only Neanderthal man but
that's another debate isn't it Seth, I guess now is not the time for the
evolutionary theories

Seth

Even if there were a unanimous decision to go against the sale or use
of genetically modified products, the case would already have been
decided without the consent of local consumers, so typically we are a
self fulfilling prophecy

Chris

An abomination before God

Seth

No Chris, what do you know about it anyway, it's a choice isn't it

Chris

A choice, yeah the choice between die now or die later, and then
come back as clone, if your good

Seth

Don't' be so ridiculous, I mean what next, you're so bloody negative

Chris

Negative or not, its' the truth

Seth

So why do you think they're having these celebrations tonight at Stereotypical?

Chris

Coz its' New Years Eve

Seth

No, coz its' a widespread search conducted by the 12 Houses to find future representatives for the Generations

Chris

So this is a sort of spot the talent night then?

Seth

Yeah, that's right, that's why they've set up this digital system on access entry, it puts the students into a selective order of categories for future references, which are to be placed on a national database

Chris

So I've got the opportunity to be selected for the 12 Houses and you just forgot to mention it?

Seth

I just did sorry forgot, anyway I thought I would surprise you

Chris

Yeah nice surprise, so what do I have to do?

Seth

Just be yourself and do what you do best

Chris

And what's that?

Seth

Looking good, while keeping quiet

Chris

Very funny, but no really Seth, who's in the running?

Seth

Well I'm all for Generation 6, as they directly went against the Liberals in the National Dome State Elections

Chris

So who or what are Generation 6 looking for?

Seth

You can't expect me to disclose all my sources of information

Chris

It sounds like you know too much already

During their conversation, Christina begins to realise and discover that Sethaniel is not being completely open and honest or transparent with her, and is concealing or deceitfully hiding some element of truth from.

Seth

Well I am already a member of the Generation 6 Youth Party

Chris

You are, since when?

Seth

Since I completed my application

Chris

Oh, I didn't know, you use to share and tell me everything before

Seth

Well just keep it to yourself

Chris

So what's your role?

Seth

I'm a junior executive on the committee

Chris

What does that mean?

Seth

It means that dealing with issues such as cross cultural links with any of my counterparts in the International Dome Youth Committees

Chris

But I thought all 3rd year minors were chosen from the 12 Houses

Seth

Well to a point that's right, but my application was submitted by a senior member of Generation 6

Chris

Yeah really, well who was that then?

Seth

Well that's not important

....

Meanwhile Joseph Blake orders a Cab and is on route and preparing to make his way to Stereotypical.

Joe

I'd like a cab please

Cabbie

Where you going mate?

Joe

I'm going to that new purpose built multi complex in the Precinct

Cabbie

What Stereotypical?

Joe

Yeah, that's it

Cabbie

Ok hop in, I'll take you there

Joe

Thanks

Cabbie

You got credit?

Joe

Well yeah I got credit, but my digital chip
appears to be malfunctioning

Cabbie

Well that's no good to me, you either got credit or you haven't

Joe

Well its' all I got, it should be working

Cabbie

Well if it isn't, then I suggest you start walking Pal

Joe

But I don't know where it is

Just then the Shuttle Cab operator notices Joseph's Angel Digital Chip.

Cabbie

Whoa wait a minute, that a left handed implant must be something new, Ok what's your Angel Digital Chip number?

Joe

Its' 147, why?

Cabbie

Well I can record it now and take a payment later, that's if I can trust you to give me the right number

Joe

Yeah that's fine, you can trust me with that, why would I lie, why would anyone lie?

Cabbie

These Shuttle cabs are equipped with the latest technology in modem travel, now put ya' hand on the screen so I can log you in to the system as a passenger

Joe

Ok man, that's cool, I appreciate it

[KEY IN DIGITAL ANGEL ICON FOR PRE PAYMENT]

Joe

ACESSING DIGITAL NUMBER 1.4.7

[FAIL – RETRY]

Joe

1.4.7. C'mon

[FAIL – RETRY]

Joe

I don't get it, its' not registering

Cabbie

That's because that's not your number, now c'mon Kid, are you playing me for some kind of fool or what?

Joe

No I'm not, seriously this is my number

Cabbie

Ok I can check it, but you ain't never seen nor laid eyes on this gadget before, you understand that

Joe

Yeah sure why, what is it, some kind of decoder?

Cabbie

Never you mind, now lets' see

[ACCESS DIGITAL ANGEL CODE 1.4.7.]

[ACCESSING DIGITAL CODE 1.4.7.......NOW OBSOLETE]

Cabbie

Please readout the current recorded digital access code

[ACCESS DIGITAL CODE UPDATE ...6.6.6]

Cabbie

Who the heck are you kid?

Joe

What do you mean, I'm me, I'm Joseph Blake

Cabbie

Well what in the hell in Satan's name is that, these numbers are classified

Joe

My name is Joe, Joseph Blake, my number is 147, I'm telling you that's the God's' honest truth

Cabbie

The truth, so what the heck do you know about it, go on keep taking then explain to me how comes you've got classified numbers on your Chip then, go on explain

Joe

I'm a student

Cabbie

Where?

Joe

1st Year University student, Dome Europe UK

Cabbie

So this is a new chip right?

Joe

Well Yes, I mean No I've had it for ages, just under a year

Cabbie

Wait a minute, you're a 1st year right?

Joe

Yeah, why?

Cabbie

So have you been anywhere abroad lately, yuh know on one of those student exchange programs?

Joe

Yeah, why?

Cabbie

Where exactly?

Joe

Dome Europe France

Cabbie

Did you buy anything?

Joe

Well yeah some relics, you know ornaments and religious symbolic antiques collectable stuff, a Bible, and stuff like that why?

Cabbie

A Bible, you actually bought a Bible, I didn't think anyone even read those books any more

Joe

Yeah well they collect en' now, why?

Cabbie

Well its' an age old thing but Bibles aren't even sold anymore, if anything they're given away freely, yuh know as presents but never sold

Joe

So what does that mean?

Cabbie

It means that whoever sold you that Bible probably picked you out as a servant, and probably got your number that way too, perhaps when you did the transaction, they could have accessed your account and credit and privacy

Joe

So what your saying is that my Digital Chip number has been hacked into and now because of that I'm A servant, a servant of what?

Cabbie

A servant of the Devil

Joe

You're kidding me right

Cabbie

No way am I kidding a Kid, its' been rumoured that a modern day occultist group are trying to bring down the new order of the 12 Houses and they will use any means necessary to gain their influence and control on the generations

Joe

So what your saying is that I've been made a disciple or a servant of this group, but its' not true, you're lying to me right, tell me this a new year prank or joke or something, you're lying right

Cabbie

I'm afraid it's' true but there must be a reason why they chose you, the only reason that I can think of, is that you possess one of the gifts of the seven seals, either that or you being exploited for some other reason, I don't know, you tell me

Joe

What seals, what gifts?

Cabbie

Its' what they call 'Black Angels

Joe

So what's a Black Angel and why the 12 Houses?

Cabbie

I've often heard tell of Black Angels and broken men who do deals and conduct business behind closed doors in order to fulfil their own ambitions and desires, so if that's what you've done or indeed what someone has done to you, maybe it is intended as a direct attempt to corrupt the 12 Houses, and implicate you to take the rap of the fall, the only one who can help you now is Obadiah 144, because if the foundations of the 12 Houses is disrupted then this reason of action against the 12, may rest upon your shoulders, I can only advise that you must try and reach Gad, as he's the only link to Obadiah 144

Joe

So what now?

Cabbie

Can I just ask you more informal inappropriate question?

Joe,

Yeah what is it?

Cabbie

Well when you went away, did you ever, yuh know get involved with anyone on a personal level

Joe

Well yes, why, is that important?

Cabbie

Well I'm not sure, could be I'm jumping to conclusions, but I'm just asking, so ya know putting two and two together, it may be a game changer, as you can't rule anything out these days

Joe

Well let's just say that I may have got lucky, but I don't quite see your point

Cabbie

Oh you will Joe, you will, now listen Joe, if that's your name and listen good, I'll take you to Stereotypical free of charge and when you get there follow all the instructions on the entry computer and key in this new digital number, and for God's sake act normal if you can do that, we have to find a way to reverse the number or the code that they've used to access your chip

Joe

Tell me again, I don't get it

Cabbie

Now pay attention, as you'll have to do as I advise you but only one of the 12 may be able to help you, the relationship between the 12 Houses and the successors of the generations which must be held together, even as we speak it is only by a thread of hope that we have not fallen upon a rock of complete chaos and disorder, that's if I haven't spoken to soon, as I feel that you may have cast a shadow of doubt on the matter, and if you are a Black Angel then know this, that by the hour you and the generations will all become broken men, you mark my words

Joe

Just tell me, will they be able to reverse the number or not?

Cabbie

Well I don't know, but you've got to get to the 12 Houses and if you do look for the one called Gad I am sure he will instruct you from there

Joe

Look for Gad

Cabbie

He'll probably find you first, but when you meet him he will give you something, maybe a stone

Joe

What kind of stone?

Cabbie

Its' a precious stone, with some magical properties it carries the resources of an insight, some kind of power, I am not sure what it does or how it works but all the houses possess one, and they are all different and they all work in a different kind of similar way, Gad will instruct you and tell you the importance and the properties of the stone but when you reach the 12 Houses, he will know you, trust me, he will know you

Joe

But I don't quite get it, Gad or the stone

Cabbie

There may be a problem when you get to Stereotypical but once you're in you may have to prove yourself, it seems that someone doesn't want you to be there for some reason in the first place, maybe you shouldn't go

Joe

Prove what?

Cabbie

Just wait and see

Joe

See what?

Cabbie

Just be ready for anything, and act like you don't know nothing, you should be good at that judging by the look of things

Joe

I don't understand

Cabbie

That's my point, but you will, now c'mon lets go

As Joseph Blake is now being driven to the precinct of Stereotypical, by his newly allied Cab Driver, he is by now somewhat agitated and disturbed by the unfolding events that he has unknowingly become subject too.

Obadiah 144

It was prophesied long ago that a true Child of nature would be born without blemish or defect and most naturally without biological and scientific interference or modification or pharmaceutical enhancement.

[SPEAK TO CONFIRM VOICE]

Joe

Hi my name is Joseph Blake, I'm 17 years old and I study at Dome Europe UK, I am very idealistic, enthusiastic, energetic as well as philosophical and forthright, many people perceive me as being restless and haunted as well as somewhat unreliable and apprehensive, I was born on the 23rd of November in London and I love the colour purple but I don't know why, I'm just really attracted to it, Any way I'm very ambitious and I love to achieve things, anything really but maybe just for the experience of life. I'm not very good at relationships but I don't like to be left on the shelf. I can be very spontaneous and assertive

I also love sports and athletics. I like to travel and I appreciate the great outdoors' as for my best attributes, which are to be friendly, honest and open minded, at present I m attending my 1st year as an undergraduate studying, Arts, Media and Cultural Studies. I would like to eventually pursue a career in Film or the Television industry or as a Teacher of Dramatic Arts, who knows possibly even as a writer or a producer of children's programmes. I am quite certain that I can achieve my aims but to me it's' not the most important thing, I think meeting the right person and bonding with them is a far greater achievement than a piece of paper or qualification that states social standing, surely I don't need this to be accepted into society, especially in a society which doesn't know itself, I think that in the future I will probably like to get married and settle down and have children but in this life that seems impossible right now so I guess it's' the just the quiet life for me, thanks

[NOW PLACE HAND OVER SCREEN AND KEY IN DIGITAL ANGEL CLASSIFICATION NUMBER]

Joe

Joseph Blake – D.O.B – 23rd NOVEMBER 2982.NO.666

ALERT........ INTEL CLASSIFIED

[SELECT LEVELS 1-12 AND DELETE AS APPRORIATE]

Joe

Levels 1-12

[LEVEL ONE-MUSIC ROOMS]
Indy-Rock-Metal-Grunge-Punk-Emo

[LEVEL TWO-MUSIC ROOMS]
Soul-Funk-Jazz-Hip Hop/Trip Hop-Electro-Grime

[LEVEL THREE-MUSIC ROOMS]
Ragga-Reggae-Ska-Lovers-Bluebeat-Jungle

[LEVEL FOUR]
Happy Hardcore-Trance-Techno
Drum n Bass-House n Garage

[LEVEL FIVE-MUSIC ROOMS]
Classical & Chamber Music

[LEVEL SIX]
Popular-Retro & Dance Music]

[LEVEL SEVEN-RELAXATION ROOMS]

Ambience Relaxation Rooms

[LEVEL EIGHT]
Smooth Chillout Lounge & Bar]

[LEVEL NINE]
Retro Chillout Rooms & Restaurant]

[LEVEL TEN]
The Arena- The Theatre
Including
-{Recitals & Discourse}
-{Poetry & Prose}

-{Characterisation & Improvisations}
-{Stand Up Comedy}
-{Acoustics & Piano}

[LEVEL ELEVEN]
The Suite / Internet Video & DVD Games-Interactive Suite
Cyber Synchronisation

[LEVEL TWELVE]
The HOUSES

[ACCESS ACKNOWLEDGED YOU
MAY ENTER LEVELS 1-12]

[ENJOY]

Just then Agent Rumsfold along with Tork of Naphtali, who
are also both currently at Stereotypical, become alerted, as a
beep sounds on his mobile device, triggered off by the arrival of
Joseph Blake's number becoming activated.

ALERT........ INTEL CLASSIFIED

Agent Rumsfold

He's here, I don't know how he did it but he's here

Tork of Naphtali

You mean Blake

Agent Rumsfold

Yes yes, now let's just find Seth and tell him that we have a bit of a problem

....

Eventually Joseph meets up with Christina and Sethaniel.

Chris

Is that Joe? Look at him, doesn't he look
the picture of health and beauty

Joe

Heya how ya doin' please, please no
introductions, just call me Joe Cool,

Chris

Joe Cool, that's so funny

Joe

Only joking Chris

Seth

Hey Joe Cool, how are you?

Joe

Seth, yeah nice one, I'm fine, and you

Seth

You don't' fool me with that cool exterior, you looked troubled, what's wrong?

Joe

No nothing, really I'm fine, I just need a drink that's all

Chris

Ok lets go and get one, Seth's been telling me all about his secrets

Seth

All my secrets, please

Chris

Well not all but its' only a matter of time
before I get the rest out of him

Seth

Your gonna have to really get me pissed before I do that
Chris

No problem, Joe what you drinking?

Joe

I'll have a root beer with ice"

Chris

And you Seth?

Seth

Whatever your having Chris

Chris

Ok two vodka and tonics and a root beer with ice coming up

Joseph follows Christina to get some drinks, in an anxious attempt to get some confirmation on what was happening to him.

Joe

Chris, I need to talk to you

Chris

What about?

Joe

About some crazy Cabbie and the 12 Houses

Chris

So what about it?

Joe

Well I don't know what's going on except that my numbers been switched, someone has messed up my number, I nearly didn't get in here tonight but the cabbie told me what to do

Chris

So what's wrong, I don't see the problem, your here aren't you

Joe

Well yeah but the cabbie started talking about the 12 or something, especially when I mentioned to him that I went to Dome Europe and bought some naff stuff, and then he started ranting on about some kind of occult

Chris

Joe something happened when you went to Dome Europe, is that what you're saying, coz right now you're just rambling on about some cab driver and not making any sense

Joe

Yeah, No, not really, well I don't know

Chris

Well calm down and tell me what you did, what happened?

Joe

I told you, this is not my number, I swear it

Chris

What's not your number, calm down, and tell me exactly what happened, what you did, where you went and try and retrace your steps

Joe

I'm trying, I can't think, help me Chris, please

Chris

How can I help you if you don't explain to me what you did

Joe

Wait a minute, when I arrived we booked into a student youth hostel and on the first day we went to the town centre to shop around and get something to eat, after that we took a sightseeing tour around the city to see some historical places, the next day …

Chris

Go on

Joe

...The next day we went to see an ancient monastery with paintings of the Madonna and child and some relics and old scriptures

Chris

Yeah but you must have touched or bought something?

Joe

No we weren't allowed to touch anything, the things were priceless and precious

Chris

Yeah but you and who, you must have touched or bought something, I don't get it

Joe

No not really, only a bible as a token of respect out of visiting the place

Chris

A Bible, you bought a bible, oh shit why!

Joe

Why what's wrong with that, your freaking me out, the cabbie said the same thing, I don't understand why is it so taboo to possess a religious book

Chris

I don't know why but you better talk to Seth about it he knows more about that kind of thing than I do

59

Joe

Yeah but the cabbie told me to keep it to myself, I wasn't even suppose to tell you about it

Chris

Well all I know is that the 12 Houses are on the top floor but you got to have access, which I don't

Joe

I've got access

Chris

Yeah but Seth said there's no need to go up there

Joe

Why not, I don't get it

Chris

Something about the Reps for the 12 Houses only go up there

Joe

Well that's what the cabbie said, you mean the Generations

Chris

Yeah that's right but anyway just check the place out and see what happens, at least you got in so it can't all be bad

Christina pays for the drinks and returns with Joseph to join Sethaniel.

Seth

Well what's going on here, private conversation or can anyone join in?

Chris

No were just deciding where to start our fun and games

Seth

Fun and games

Joe

Yeah

Seth

Yeah right pull the other one, its' got bells on it, I see you two are as thick as thieves, I know your concocting something together, better watch her Joe, when she's unleashed there's no stopping her, go on hurry up Chris and get back in your box

Just then Seth laughs to himself as they all walk over to a glass elevator in one corner of the ground floor building, and as they enter, Seth presses the elevator button.[LEVEL EIGHT] Smooth Chillout Lounge & Bar] Going Up

Chris

Yeah what, what do you mean exactly Seth

Seth

Something's going up, that's all I know, Oh C'mon yuh know, sex, sex and more sex to be precise

Chris

Sex! I don't see sex as a leisure's activity for your pastime pleasure you know Seth

Seth

Yeah right, like you've never done it in public places, so where don't you like doing instead, c'mon?

Chris

I like to make love, instead, if you get my drift

Seth

Make love, so what is the difference, your only saying that coz
Joe's knocking about, your such a hypocrite Chris, making love,
that's absurd, blah blah blah, love, I wonder if you've even got any
emotions to discard, love, don't make me laugh

Joe

Well sorry Seth, but the way you say it,
makes it sound filthy and dirty

Seth

Well that's coz that's what it is, isn't it, its' animalistic, were all
beasts of the jungle, shagging each other to death and loving every
minute of it

Joe

Well that's the way you see it, but to me it's' more than that, much
more, and I disagree with your crude remarks about it, maybe you're
an animal but my sexual obsession are not made up of games and
base deeds Seth, I think you're the beast,

Chris

Yeah Seth, you're the beast and I'm the beauty, I think making love
is best experienced in soul music, its' so soft and sensual and so
romantic, it makes you feel as if your being pulled into a world of
deep hypnosis, I like to feel loved and appreciated and the music

63

reinforces that emotion, I want to be whisked off my feet and penetrated softly until I come, and then I want to be held until the feeling inside subsides and you daydream

Joe

No shit, that's the business, that's what I'm talking about, making love to music, maybe not soul but some deep shit, like Chicago Electro or Jazz or Rock even

Seth

I bet that music burns a lot of friction

Joe

Yeah your right but its' still making love instead of Wham Bam thank you Mam!

Seth

Well let's just say for real taste, a glass of Wine, some classical music, and yes, perhaps a cigarette, and then followed by that nocturnal art of pretending to fall asleep whilst fondling to feed the appetite

Chris

No, No! You wanna be held, until you know that you've expressed and shared, and then something special happens, something wonderful now that's the business

Seth

The business, more like pure fantasy, you don't know what making love is, your just dramatists, romanticists, both of you, I mean imagine sex and taking in the act or oral exploration and using sex toys and bondage it just gets deeper and deeper

Chris

Nice, you mean like incense and body oils and your favourite ice cream spread all over your body

Seth

Yeah licked off with a sensual tongue, now that's pleasure unparallel, that's the shit, I remember I read in a psychology journal, that in a study of human behaviour, that Freud said 'that from the age of five that every point of human contact we experience is based on a sexual interpretation' and that's why some men and women have such a high and uncontrollable sexual urges, wait for it, the libido, Oh, yes I rest my case, the gravitational pull is all sex, sex, and more sex

Chris

Yeah but Freud was a nymphomaniac, I bet he probably shagged the arse off all his patients, I mean you don't' you just love drawing conclusions like that from the point of observation, I bet you he probably shagged the men too, ya know, just to be certain

Joe

Yeah Freud's a nutter, imagine shagging at the age of five

Seth

I wasn't' saying that, your both exaggerating and twisting my point with your dirty little minds, Freud's a brilliant minded psychologist, he freed our libido on the subject of human behaviour, even if he was bisexual

Joe

Was he!

Chris

Oh shut up Joe, Mr bright and gullible

Seth

So what are you two up to, are you staying on this level all night?

Chris

I don't' know, whatever

Seth

What about you Joe?

Joe

I'm not sure

Seth

So why don't we check out the Cyber Synchronisations room, do you wanna come along with me upstairs, yuh know, checkout the chandeliers and all that jazz?

Joe

What me, now!

Seth

Yeah now, c'mon on, what about you Chris?

Chris

I think I'm gonna get drunk and think about leaving when the postman comes

Joe

What's that suppose to mean?

Seth

I think it means she's leaving in the morning, in coma, when the neon lights stop spinning and twinkling

Chris

So everyone's going upstairs for a bit of the other then

Seth

Of course they are, that's where all the fun and games are, are you coming Joe?

Joe

No I'm not, I just thought that you were kidding…

Chris

Well that's what you get for thinking, kidding I mean

Seth

Why don't you come up and have a look, you might learn something new Joe

Chris

Stop teasing him Seth

Seth

I'm not, I'm just egging him on a bit, yuh know Dutch courage and all that, I mean he's got to get with the programme sometime Chris

Just then Seth pulls out a rolled up cigarettes and lights it up and takes a few puffs and then offers it to Joe.

Seth

Here Joe, why don't you take a couple of puffs on this, nobody's watching, nobody really cares in here anyway

Joe

What is it?

Seth

Its' just a joint, yuh know Marijuana

Joe

No thanks Seth

Seth

C'mon Joe enjoy yourself

Joe

No!

Seth

C'mon, what's the matter?

Chris

Leave him Seth he's alright, do you want another drink Joe?

Joe

Yeah alright, I'll have another root beer

Sethaniel starts to approach Joseph and touch him inappropriately. Joe shrugs Seth off from putting his arms around his shoulder

Seth

What's the matter with you, why so tense, c'mon on enjoy yourself

Joe

I said I want a root beer

Christina gets in-between Joseph and Sethaniel.

Chris

Stop pissing people off Seth

Seth

Alright no need to get your knickers in a twist

Chris

If you weren't such a pansy I would have decked you by now

Seth

No violence please, especially coming from a girl like you, oh I forget, it must be time to get the claws out

Chris

Your cruisin' for a brusin' now go on toddle off and do as your told and get the drinks in, mines a glass of wine, red or white will do, after all its' only a piss up

....

As Angel Ruen arrived upon the Dome, for a moment there was a sudden surge of an electrical charge, causing a blackout of all the electrical and digital connections to short circuit momentarily, bringing about complete darkness as he had descended upon the precinct where Stereotypical was situated, as it was during this temporary shutdown, that Angel Ruen discretely entered into the complex unnoticed and undetected, and was by now readily seeking out the one known as Obadiah 144, as shortly after, did the backup systems reboot and everything was restored once more to full functionality.

Seth

Wow what was that, did you notice that

Chris

Yeah, didn't the lights just go out or flicker or something,

Joe

I think it was a short circuit

Chris

I'll short circuit you in a minute Joe

Seth

Madam please the language, better watch out Joe, the mouth on it, she's onto you ya know

Chris

You can talk Seth

Seth

Ok I'm going now, your both such boring farts, I think the two of you were made for each, have fun wont you, now cheers me dears.

....

Obadiah 144 continues to make his recordings, as the events at Stereotypical continue to unfold and develop.

Obadiah 144

As it was prophesied that all flesh shall fall away, and yet all souls shall be gathered up together, and all spirits shall rise and be carried away by the vestiges and the virtues of the Angels coming forth out of Heaven, and yet even in this eventuality Mankind has not prepared himself for his departure from this World, but instead, insist on building Vessels and Outposts in the regions of space to carry himself forever forward into the new worlds of discovery awaiting, and yet so it is, that I Obadiah 144 shall also serve to influence and to guide this mortal transition and end the days of journeying, beyond such futile aspirations to a positive conclusion, and yet that which is not of God shall also perish and be found to be no more of an expression in these Universal threads of life, but as life and death, which are not a matter of choice, but rather a pardonable forgiveness or condemnation by the living spirit, then so let it be that if all flesh is found to be unfit and without the properties of the spirit, then what is there to be salvaged and saved for this new World, as for the Earth is to be restored back to the fullness of her glory, then so the soul of Mankind must be uprooted and made to serve out an equivalence of his birthright within the Heavens, until such time as the restoration is complete and fulfilled, and the soul of Man is ignited once more by the living spirit amongst the stars and planted like seeds upon the Earth.

....

As they both sit talking in the chillout rooms, Christina attempts to make a romantic pass and advancement towards Joseph and then begins to entice him.

Chris

So Joe do you wanna dance with me?

Joe

Dance, I can't dance, I've got two left feet

Chris

What do ya mean you can't dance, anyone can dance, just move to the music, c'mon I'll show you

Joe

No seriously, I can't Chris

Chris

Just hold me, and I'll help you

Joe

Okay, Alright

Chris

Seth's quite the entertainer, but he can be a bit too much sometimes don't you think

Joe

Yeah he can

Chris

C'mon put your hands round my waist, pull me tighter, that's it, tighter, c'mon closer, closer, that's it

Joe

Is Seth gay?

Chris

Seth, he's a right funny one, why are you?

Joe

No! Why are you?

Chris

I'm a good girl, I wouldn't do a thing like that, beside I love boys too much, anyway I though you knew about Seth

Joe

Well sort of, but I wasn't sure

Chris

Seth likes anything with a hole in it, he's a bit high on life, and he' a randy little gigolo, look at him, he fancies anything that can walk but he never gets any

Joe

Gets any what?

Chris

Love, Sex, he never gets any true love out of it, it's all pleasure games with Seth, in the toilets, back seat of a car, butt naked up on the common, anywhere different, that's' our Seth, and he loves to kiss and tell… so tell me Joe, do you wanna dance in private or what?

Christina takes Joseph by the hand and leads him to a more secure place inside the venue and starts to seduce him.

Joe

What do ya mean, where?

Chris

You know what I mean, c'mon come upstairs, follow me

Joe

There's something I need to tell you

Chris

What's that Joe?

Joe

Oh it doesn't matter

Chris

C'mon what is it, oh no wait a minute, I think I know, its' alright, calm down, now c'mon here's an empty room, we can dance in here together, it'll be fun, now I can show you how its' done properly... c'mon touch me properly, don't be afraid, no one's watching us anyway

Joe

What!

Chris

Touch me...touch me here, I know you want too, c'mon don't be shy

Joseph starts to relax, as he begins to caress Christina.

Joe

What here?

Chris

Yeah, go on unclip me then

Joe

Are you sure?

Chris

Are you?

Joe

I can't get it undone

Chris

Come here and let me do it, you get undressed, c'mon now quick before Seth gets back

Joe

What in here', what if someone…

Chris

Its' alright, they won't, you haven't gone this far before have you?

Joe

Well yes, I mean no, well my last female friend wanted to take things slow

Chris

Did you love her?

Joe

Yeah in a way I did, she was nice

Chris

Nice! Is that it

Joe

Yeah, she was really nice, she said I was a man of heart, we use to talk a lot about the future

Chris

So what about it, all heart or all man

Joe

What?

Chris

The future Joe, what about it, you seem so distant and distracted, what's wrong with you?

79

Joe

Oh, we were gonna live abroad, maybe buy a property in Dome Europe somewhere, well that was her fantasy anyway, except that she's from a completely different House to me, so ya know we couldn't really be together in the end anyway, not really, not for keeps sake anyway, especially when you really think about it

Chris

So what happened then?

Joe

When?

Chris

At the Dome Europe, the villa, Italy, Spain, you and your girlfriend, what happened?

Joe

Well she got a scholarship to study foreign languages overseas somewhere, Dome International, so we split, but we planned to stay in touch and get together if things changed, but I don't know what happened really, it was all over so quickly

Chris

Do I turn you on?

Joe

Yeah, you do

Chris

Are you hard now, I want you too…

Joe

Oh that feels really good, you want me to what

Chris

Slowdown tiger, you're getting a bit too excited, I want you too pullout when you think you're ready to come okay

Just then Joseph and Christina begin having sexual intercourse inside a remote corner of one of the chillout rooms.

Joe

Chris, oh shit, Chris…

Chris

Slow Joe, slowly, and when you pullout, I
want you to come all over me

Joe

...Oh shit, I'm coming

Chris

C'mon quick, pullout

Joe

I am

Chris

C'mon, come here and put your coat over me, I love it, your shivering, let me hold you and warm you up a bit

Joe

Its' quite exciting, I have never come like that before but, wow! That was amazing

Chris

I can' believe it, you was inside me, was it like that with her

Joe

No, with my girlfriend it was different

Chris

But I thought you haven't done it before

Joe

Well I haven't, well maybe once or twice, but I use to come in my
trousers, every time she laid on top of me, it was in the dark, I just
did what came naturally

Chris

Premature ejaculation, what a waste of resources, well its better
than interactive cyber synchronisation sex I guess, anyway as far as
I know we don't even have periods anymore or produce any fertile
eggs anymore, and clones can't hardly secrete any semen, so in my
book that makes you one of a kind, even more special, so never mind
eh', maybe next time I want you in my mouth next time, and I want
you to know what it tastes like, so what was her name

Joe

Who, Oh you mean Mary

Chris

Oh your all soft now, but its' alright, I can soon rectify that, they
say that the second time lasts longer, then we can really make love,
whichever you prefer

Joe

Your pretty good at this

Chris

Well let's just say I'm more experienced at it than you are, how does it feel Joe?

Joe

I'm not quite sure but the bloods rushing to my head, I guess it feels quite good

Chris

I want you to do one thing for me

Joe

What's that?

Chris

Forget all about Mary and go down on me Joe

Joe

Go down on you! Are your serious

Chris

Am I serious, well yeah of course I am, you do know what to do don't you, just let your tongue do all the talking and imagine that you're looking for a cherry buried in ice cream, they say that eventually you find what you're looking for

Joe

Cherries and ice cream, sounds nice, how am I doing?

Chris

That's' fine, it feels so good, keep doing it, make me come Joe, make me come

Joe

I can see that this is gonna be deep with you, so what do you want me to

Chris

I think there's more to you than meets the eye

Joe

Do you?

Chris

I do, I wish I could be like you

Joe

Why what's that?

Chris

Free...you're quite a thinker, aren't you?

Joseph tries to break away, but Christina holds onto him.

Joe

I don't know, I suppose I am, come on we should dance some more?

Chris

I'll have to think about that, the first one was a present from me to you but now that I know what you're thinking, I'm gonna have to be more careful how I play my cards

Joe

I love you yuh know

Christina suddenly pushes Joseph away.

Chris

What, what the hell are you saying, you're talking crap your such a soap box

Joe

No I do, I really do Chris

Chris

Yeah right, do you really think that five minutes of frolicking suddenly turns into a full blossomed romance, I don't think so Joe, you're sick, hopeless, absolutely frigging hopeless

Joe

But Chris I want you, I want to be with you properly, but not like this, you know properly

Chris

You just had me, and now you just blew it

Joe

No what I meant to say is that I wanted to be with you, but there's something going on, I can't explain it

Chris

Look five minutes ago you were a virgin and now suddenly you're a man, I can't believe it, Man of heart Joe, more like a hopeless romantic, your just a boy Joe

Joe

What?

Chris

Lighten up Joe, and just relax and enjoy yourself, parties are always like this

Joseph gets slightly frustrated and annoyed.

Joe

What like this, mad, crazy, funny!

Chris

Yeah, mad, crazy, fun, nothing serious Joe

Joe

I can be mad, crazy if you want to be, mad, crazy, funny even

Chris

So what's stopping you?

Joe

Nothing, I just wanna be with you, with no one else around

Chris

There you go again, you're being so serious, so what was Mary a virgin or something then

Joe

Well yeah, she was from Dome Europe, a different House but a first year like me, but, I met here on the exchange programme

Chris

Well to be honest Joe, I think I'm too much women for you even on a good day, maybe this Mary friend of yours felt the same way you do, but I don't do love, I just like it nice and simple

Joe

Maybe you don't know love Christina, and maybe you're not as serious as Mary, but at least gimme a chance

Chris

A chance to do what Joseph Blake, to blow sweet nothings in my ear, your just an air head, a dreamer, Seth's opinion of you was so spot on

Joe

Please Chris, at least let me show you what I feel is true

Chris

How can you feel anything, feel what is it with you, its shit, were clones, how are we suppose to feel love, tell me then, what is it, what do you possesses that no one else does eh tell me that

Joe

Well to be honest, I don't think that I was

Chris

That you wasn't what, what Cloned, but that's ridiculous, just listen to yourself so what you so bloody perfect and above everyone else now or something

Joe

Just hear me out Chris, I'm being for real, its' not about what we just did, I wanted you before that, I just didn't know how to tell you, but you made it simple, something that I felt with Mary, I didn't feel with you, I never really knew who she was, or why we even met, but we did, and now I don't know or anything or even why, things just don't make any sense anymore

Chris

Seriously, and I thought you were just being shy, are you that disconnected from the planet, that you just ain't got a clue

Joe

I am, its' just that you're so straightforward, that I didn't need to tell you until now

Chris

So you find my conversation a little bit offensive and in ya face then?

Joe

Well yeah its' a little bit awkward, but that's you isn't it

Chris

So you don't know if you were cloned or not, so there is actually a man in there somewhere after all, but he's now tongue tied, is that right

Joe

Well just because I approach things differently, doesn't meant that you have to use such a vicious language to hide your insecurities, it doesn't have to be put like that...

Chris

Vicious language!

Joe

It's not a joke Chris

Chris

A joke, yeah like I'm really laughing but you haven't said anything amusing since we started talking, I don't believe it, Seth wants it both ways, I'm competing with a Virgin, and you're so straight its' almost clinically stupid beyond ridicule, I don't know if I should hug you or send you off to join the rest of the boring in crowd…, so what was she all about then

Joe

Who?

Chris

Your ex-girlfriend, Mary, the so called female perfect match idyllic friend of yours

Joe

Mary, Mary was just Mary, in a way were both the same, maybe in a way too much, and maybe too similar

Chris

Mary was Mary, don't make me laugh, I can see that you were both quite an exceptional virginal couple

Joe

That's not funny, I think we better go find Seth, there's no telling what trouble he's getting into right now

Chris

No more than us I suppose

Joe

Yeah

Chris

Are you alright, you look disappointed, like you've disappeared into some dark corner of your mind

Joe

I just thought, it felt different that's all, it felt nice

Chris

What, what we just did?

Joe

Well yeah, to be with you, to touch you, I felt special, that's why I said what I said

Chris

I know why you said it Joe, but its' easy to say it Joe, isn't it, its' so bloody easy and convenient to say it, and even if you mean it, I still wouldn't want you to prove it, you couldn't anyway, and your hardly experienced in the sexual department, so maybe you should go talk to Seth, he'll tell you a thing or two about it, and no doubt when Seth finds out that your more natural than the rest of us, he'll have a field day with you

Joe

Seth! Why Seth?

Chris

Why do ya think?

Joe

You're kidding, Seth! What Seth and me?

Chris

Yeah you and Seth, he wants you something Chronic

Joe

You're Kidding, I can't... I'm not

Chris

I know Joe, you're not gay, your just ridiculous, now I know why they didn't clone you, but I mean it, Joe, he wants your arse for breakfast, dinner and lunch

Joe

Well he can't even ave' me for a snack, no way Chris, no way

Chris

Why not, what's wrong with it?

Joe

Well it's just not me

Chris

Oh it isnt' is it

Joe

Its' not, not where I'm concerned, I mean he's alright as a mate, I care about Seth but not like, you understand that Chris, don't you?

Chris

Alright like you care, about zilch, zero about Mary, that's a laugh, so tell me what is it all about Joe, why don't you tell me, deep down coz I think that you're a control freak or insecure or something like that, you've got real issues with your tissues

Joe

Why say that, is that what you think I believe

Chris

Belief, So what! Is that what's it all about then, what Joe, what don't you wanna see people like me or Seth have a great time enjoying ourselves, well life goes on regardless, and Seth and I don't care about it, so why should you?

Joe

Because I do

Chris

Because you do, but do you, suddenly you're the best thing since cloning began, I think your just like all the other male chauvinist pigs in here Joe, I really do

Joe

What's that suppose to mean?

Chris

You just care about yourself and your afraid to let go and you can't
bear to be a part of something that you don't understand

Joe

No Chris, its' not true

Chris

Well what about Seth, do you think you understand him because
I don't think you do…Oh what's wrong now, are we feeling a wee
little bit insecure now Joe, just go, why don't you just go

Joe

Are you suggesting that I'm homophobic or something?

Chris

I'm not suggesting it because quite clearly you are, more like
clonophobic

Christina starts to laugh out loud to herself.

Joe

I'm not

Chris

You are

Joe

Don't mess with my mind Chris, I don't have to sit here and defend my principles to you, or to Seth, or to anyone

Chris

Alright calm down, I was only winding you up, it doesn't matter to me Joe, I don't care what they dream up, or try to control us with, they call it Dome democracy but it aint' is it, and to tell you the truth I don't want to get married to anyone, I don't want children who are practically programmed to do as their told, I mean who in their right minds wants to bring clones into this world, I think your girlfriend was right in letting you go, your insane, do you really want to bring Genetics into a world like this, you're a bloody fantasist a complete hopeless romantic and I mean it Joe you really are

Joe

Now wait a minute Chris…hang on

Chris

No you hang on, just accept it and move on, its' not gonna change not now, not ever, were still young, you should get some experience and live life a little bit more, who knows maybe you'll look back at it all in a different way, maybe in your 3rd year perhaps you'll meet Mrs

Right, if the system so desires, even if she happens to be computer cloned handpicked or made to measure mail order, you'll be satisfied

Joe

Your soul mate is inside you Chris no matter who is beside you, you obviously lack a little bit of faith

Chris

Faith yeah right, what do you want with faith, even now as we speak the computers are mapping out our charts, God knows it's' activated every seven days and goes out to a central database all over the world, it picks our jobs, it selects our life partners, it determines where we should live, all this is calculated according to Health, Wealth, Colour, technical ability and Whatever Generation you happen to come under, so don't get frustrated with me or Seth and enjoy your life, you've only got two more years of freedom so enjoy it and I'm sure you'll meet that perfect whatever thing-a-mi-jig type of girl fantasy that you dream off

Joe

Sagittarius, she'll be Sagittarian

Chris

Sagittarian, yeah I'm sure she's out there in the system somewhere

Joe

Do you think that the system is influenced by the 12 divisions of the Houses, I mean why are the Generations so important, it makes sense now, it makes us remain obedient in an orderly fashion, I suppose it's not completely crap but I wish I could love and marry anyone, someone of my own choosing, I mean at the end of the day surely if it doesn't matter who your friends are then it shouldn't apply if you love someone, and if you want to procreate, then its' compulsory that your partner has to be from the same House, that's the part I don't get, I mean its' stupid, who would design something like that, why?, ya know looking back I think the real reason why me and my girlfriend split up is because she was very ambitious and I didn't despise her of wanting to make a success of her life, and maybe because of this blasted system, she knew it wouldn't work, she did me a favour, I knew it, whenever they mentioned the alternative methods of maternal, paternal reproduction, she thought it crazy, she even said it was insane and that we shouldn't think about it, I mean for someone as intellectual as she was, she seemed to be quite naive on the subject on the whole, and although I'm not totally against the system, its' only now I begin to realise even more, but surely we can choose can't we?

Chris

We can choose nothing, the choosing and the choices are made for us

Just then Sethaniel returns, looking very pleased and confident with himself.

100

Seth

Hi I'm back, I was thinking about getting back to basics ya know, the whole point of being focussed on myself was to create a healthy steady lifestyle, ya know of sound mind and body and all that, well anyway it seems to me that you get accused of being self centred, ya know what I mean people become obsessed and possessive not only with themselves but they actually think they own you, you know 'Simon says' and all that, it seems inescapable so why can't my world revolve around me a little and my ideals and not the people who require my time as you two do, I just want to evolve, or maybe they think I'm a vegetable or something but surely I'm just as needy as what they are aren't I ?, you see there it is I automatically fall into the trap of self analysis, fuck it, I hate it, its' all a contradiction which kicks you in the teeth with a metal toecap boot and that's just to add to my troubles, so what have you two been up to?

Chris

Ask him

Joe

Just talking, ya know catching up

Seth

Do you know I've discovered they've got a cybersex room, do you wanna try it out, its' completely interactive with automated sensory impulses, I can even feel you come inside me, imagine that, sex without exchanging bodily fluids, man that's got to be the ultimate turn for any playmate

Joe

Come off it Seth your sex mad, I'm not doing that shit

Seth

What do ya mean surely you must have wondered what it would be like with a real man Joe

Joe

No flipping way Seth, I'm strictly hetero

Seth

C'mon on Joe you won't be converted, trust me its' all in the mind, I promise you, c'mon please, trust me, I wanna feel you, I wanna taste you, I want to feel the experience, c'mon Joe knock yourself out do it for me

Joe

Why me, why don't you just choose someone else, and get them to do it, I'm sure there's loads of fellas looking for a good time, with a real man, besides if you were a real man surely you'd do the natural thing and find yourself a real woman

Seth

Yeah alright enough already, I just wanted to try it out with a mate, I thought you would be game, I know you, I Know what you're like you're just afraid you might just like it

Joe

Well you can either ask Christine or you can pick someone else, but there's no way you're getting me hooked up on some cyber machine, just so you can have some fun, coz I also know what you're like Seth, your just up for anything well friends or no friends, I'm not having it and that's final

Chris

Alright you two, enough of the ego's clashing and testosterone flying all around, just calm down, as your both having a negative effect on my karma, I actually hate getting annoyed with my friends, and its' the worst feeling in the world to be angry and upset with the people closest to you, its' like losing a piece of yourself, maybe we should attend classes in emotional anger management, ya know for letting it all hang out when it really counts, and then you can get pissed off with things that really matter, like fighting the system and becoming the tomorrow people instead of swallowing these ideological theories they keep feeding us, sue the Houses, I'm not here to be taken for a ride, you get more human rights if you're a monkey in a laboratory cage, I want my own state of independence, your right in a way Joe, they actually set it up in a way so that the victim is the person in the wrong, the crazy, insane, wicked little elected leaders that, control, control, and reinforce control, that's all they know, and to think they dreamt this shit up, but yuh know the beautiful thing about it is, is that it would be so brilliant, if we wasn't' on the losing end, right guys

Seth

You can speak for yourself Chris,

Joe

What's that suppose to mean?

Seth

As a general rule…

Chris

…As a general rule you've got to know where you stand, that's why I sort of believe in Angels and all that, but I think that God is a bit different, he doesn't actually intervene if he thinks your death will make a difference, he won't mind using you as a sacrifice, he's not bad or wicked or anything like that, but its' all fated, its' our histories that we need to be made examples of, that's why in Gods plans everyone's expendable, that's why I like Angels because if they can help you they will coz they're Gods subjects and they've also got a vested interest in what happens to us, because it affects them too, so I don't choose isolation as a form of defence because that's where the spirits come into you, and you don't know whether your entertaining good or bad ones, wicked or evil ones, remember safety in numbers, its' all true but you have to be disciplined and concentrate on your immediate future needs, because people come…

Seth

…And people go and if its' not about you, then what is it about after all were all special, I see you remembered

Chris

Yeah, amazing stuff Seth

Joe

Well I think we need to divert away from these outwardly vanities and realise its' time to wake up and smell the coffee, the focus of our attention is not necessarily written in the stars, but is somewhere between an inwards journey and our own external universe fusing together, this is the central connection which brings us peace, love and understanding of ourselves, even if others doubts us, at least by our present we are still not separated from beyond our own spheres of influence, but we must realise that the body is dying and life is the master and living is the lesson, it is the spirit that is the true master of the human condition, and not us

Seth

You make it all sound so clinically perfectible

Chris

That doesn't sound like you Joe, its' not what you were saying before

Joe

Yeah but your version sounds so surreal and unobtainable, but to look at it another way, all is fair in love, which goes to show that this goes equally hand in hand with peace and happiness, if that is to say that in an idealist view, but in this world they take all the spoils of war in order to create a perfect world but instead it results in all the abominations that we witness today, so do you really expect to have an angelic enlightened mind or heart, when we construct society this way, what is there to understand, understand what, what the hell do we understand from that, I could really go to town on the subject but it breaks me down just to think about it, I'm too weak to take action on a personal level but it is isn't it, it's a personal, thing to everyone, to all of us, all of us trying to understand, to make, and to take and to create and even dictate a perfect philosophy for living, and then in the process we mess it all up, bloody marvellous, so what do we do, do we keep going round in a repetitive circle until we die

Seth

Ya know what Joe your more civilised that anyone in this crummy little joint, look at em' all strawberries and cream, its' about time that I injected some fun into this party, don't you think

Just then Christina begins to feel cautiously aware and somewhat uncomfortable with everything going on around them.

Chris

Seth, that bloke over there keeps giving you the eye

Seth

I know, I saw him earlier, I'm so obvious

Joe

What bloke?

Seth

Never mind, its' not important

Chris

I think he's up for it

Joe

What with you?

Seth

Yeah he wants me, don't be so surprised Joe, wait a here a minute, I'm just gonna check him out, I might get his number

Unknowingly to Christina and Joseph who this stranger might be, Seth walks over to Agent Rumsfold, and speaks with him for a brief moment before returning.

Seth

He's so completely, boring, with no personality, and no depth

Joe

Seth I'm not at all easily surprised at your exaggerated remarks, I know that you know I will accept just about anything that you say without disregard or judgement, but I do reject your corruptible notions and schoolboy antics, I think it's' about time you adopted a more sensible attitude, if that is humanly possible

Seth

I can assure you Joe, that the devil is not gay, in fact I think he's far to intelligent for that, don't you agree, in fact I would even go as far as calling him a loser, as I do believe he doesn't even masturbates, why do you?

Chris

Seth, that's out of order

Joe

Don't worry about it Chris, I'm totally open to anything that may be a deliberate attempt to liberate my sexuality, but seeing as its' expressed with such precise wisdom and humour then it is only water off a ducks back so to speak

Seth

You such a wish one Joe, you saw right through me, didn't you, I like you the more I get to know you, please forgive me for my schoolboy antics, although I can be quite a patronising contemptuous little sod, but I do believe, that honestly the first step to hallowed be thou heaven is to accept anything that this world throws at you, as I also think that your well on your way to overcoming such uninventive insanity, be it man made or God divine, I can see were both alike you and I

Joe

Yeah and I can see where going nowhere fast

Chris

Going nowhere fast

Seth

No, no, were venturing out, out there somewhere, anywhere

Joe

I think this idea of similarities or any one of us as being the same is uninventive insanity, whether it be to change, or not to change, that is the question, misrepresentation or miscommunication, I mean who wants to sell out to this rule of, just act like me, or just talk like me and do everything I do kind of bullshit, thinking everything will be alright with our heads buried in the sand, its' absurd, not one of us is prepared for the culture shock or the genesis of perfection of any kind of genius because it all cracks up in the end, to think we want every version written in blood as a testimonial, every action reproduced or assimilated, every interpretation updated, that got everyone going, didn't it, do it by the letter or were gonna fail, and if we fail, then it won't work, whether we agree or disagree, its' all compulsory, its' absolutely necessary but their always gonna need someone to crack open a can of ideas just like us cracking perfection right now

Seth

Don't you feel better now that you've got that off your mind, does it make you feel like your someone now, don't you think

Chris

Yeah, I think the moody, broody stuff is boring, but I can see that Joe thinks about a lot of things

Seth

But it's' not wise Joe, you'll get ill and depressed if you're not careful, always remember to resurface and come up for air, for Christ sake man, don't' be so serious all the time, its' not you, this is your big chance to take every opportunity to be open minded about things, that's what I like about you, c'mon on then, do things to me, anything, anything you like, hurt me, hurt me Joe, I don't mind, I want you to be inventive, be imaginative, use your mind, use your body, I'll be whatever you want

Joe

Stop it! Just stop it there, I don't want this, I don't want anything, its' not right, its' not what I'm into, I had you all wrong, I thought you were a mate, now I know you're not just acting up, you're so fake, its' all false, its' all a game to you, Seth stop playing these games, if you think that I believe that gaining someone's trust or friendship or respect is based on what tricks they can perform for me, then its' not right and you know it Seth, its' not right, if all you wanna do is have sex and manipulate your friends then you can count me out and just stop assuming that all men and women want to sleep with you, you had me wrong from the word go, that's where were different, I don't play those games, and even if I knew how too I don't think I would, so yeah like you were saying there has gotta be a better outcome than just constantly getting shit on by the system, but if that's how it is for you then I'm out of here, see ya around Seth, see ya Chris, no doubt you wanna hang around with the likes of him and get insulted all night

Seth

Well excuse me, my apologies for hurting ones sensitivities

....

As the Moon with all its moonbeams which had once decorated the midnight Sky like a distant satellite, long after the Sun had first risen upon its' Eastern horizon flaring out sunrays over the Dome on that New Years' Eve Day, as it was somewhat of an inevitable unexpected phenomenon, that along with the days

events' now found to be unfolding, that the Sun upon its setting on the Western horizon, that so too in the Heavens above did the Angels of the Celestial Abode led by the Angel of Mercy and the Angel of Justice at opposite ends of this spectrum, begin their approach to the newly polarised Celestial Equator, if not for some strange and profound reason upon the laws of creation, which was by now influencing these Angels of Heaven, to take up aligned positions along this Celestial Orbit of Polaris the North Star in the Constellation of Ursa, and also upon Octans, the Southern Star in the constellation of Sigma Octantis if only in order to become prepared and ready to descend upon the Dome.

....

And so it was that Angel Ruen wandered around this unsuspecting crowd of Stereotypical, who seemed somewhat rather oblivious to this Angel of Heaven, whose surreal appearance seem to fit in perfectly, as it may very well have been assumed by any onlookers that he were dressed appropriately for this occasion, as it was upon this most elaborate and spectacular costume of display, that as many other people were also dressed up in such exaggerated and flattering attire within this unusual environment in which he had found himself, and which also lent itself in disguising him against the backdrop of an accommodating fashion of expression for this celebration and activity, and so he was naturally perceived and marvelled upon as a distinguished subject in such an amazing display of the proceedings which was consistent with this time of year, and yet Angel Ruen was simply left to watch and observe as such crowds of flamboyant individuals came and went about their sociable and pleasurable experiences.

Joe

Excuse me, I'm sorry, I didn't mean to bump into like that, I wasn't looking where I was going

An Innocent

Its' alright it was my fault entirely, I thought you were someone else

Joe

Oh that's' alright, I was wondering can you tell me how you get access to see any members of the 12 Houses?

An Innocent

The Houses, have you got access?

Joe

Well yes, but I don't know which is the House of Gad

An Innocent

Well they say ignorance is to arrogance what naivety is to innocence, there are many strings to one bow yuh know, but that is to say that in this world there are one of two things and they are the programmed and the programmer or the influenced and the influencer, the question is which are you?

Joe

Who am I, Who are you?

An Innocent

I am the same as you, now think about it carefully as I am only interested in the future progressive state of being or at least something more utopian other than just another police state, do you follow my drift, because God is a creature of inexplicable parts and great complexities, he or she is not to be perceived as being just an idol deity, we are in fact scientist and God is a master of illusion if not the most exceptional and greatest miracle worker like ever

Joe

But who is God?

An Innocent

Who is God, you mean you don't know who God is, well ask yourself this one question, has anyone ever met with the great illusionist of nothing, has anyone even ever seen or understood it, even though its' there and everywhere to be seen and to be felt

Joe

Well yeah, I suppose with the power or
perception anything is possible

114

An Innocent

Of course it requires the power of perception and if we deviate from God then we lose the power, simple, but you know I told God the other day that he or she should be very specific, and very precise in his or her instruction and allow no room for conjecture or suppositions

Joseph becomes somewhat confused and dumbfounded by this strange conversation that is taking place between himself and this Innocent stranger.

Joe

You know God!

An Innocent

Yes of course I know God, everyone knows God, don't be stupid, now try not to deviate from your path as I was trying to tell you I asked God for a sign and he presented me with you

Joe

Are we talking about the same person I don't quite understand

An Innocent

Yes we are, you see Gad is Gad which is whom you are seeking, and God is God, who of course in the master illusionist, but I can see that you are on a borderline between the tainted and the innocent, as this paradox of truth worries you, and it should too, but to be confused is not a good medium, so let me begin by counteracting your instability, but firstly you must follow my instruction by reading this leaflet which will also help you to understand

Joe

Oh what is it an invitation to a temple or something

An Innocent

No! Just read

Joseph takes the piece of paper and begins to read it.

We believe that Tork of Capricorn from the House of Napthali leaked a dossier to an agent named Rumsfold which apparently contained some confidential information on a 'trans symmetry altered states imagem technique which was being developed by Generation 7 and it seems that Rumsfold is planning to steal theses plans for Generation 6

Joe

So why come to me?

An Innocent

Because not only are you an innocent like me but you are also a link, that is why they are trying to taint and discredit you

Joe

How come you know this

An Innocent

Because your chosen

Joe

So what do I have to do?

An Innocent

Why don't you try by e-mailing Gad on 'Gods Great Computer' in the internet suite, just tap in Mark Of Man.Com, Gads always on line for a chat, he's a nice man you'll like him

Joe

World Wide Web, Triple Six Dot Com you say?

An Innocent

Yeah that's right followed by the mark of man, its' alright I know how you feel, it sort of hits like a sudden fear completely gripping your senses and leaving you feeling as cold as ice, its' fight or flight time but your curiosity is thirsty to know more answers and you're as scared as hell but they say better the devil you know than the devil you don't

Joe

Yeah that's exactly what I'm feeling

An Innocent

So tell me in all honesty, what is the greatest of all your fears, what is the worst thing that can happen?

Joe

I don't know, I hate to think about it

An Innocent

Well look at it this way you in control of your destiny so it can't all be bad and you're a nice guy, so don't forget it now be a man and go have a talk with Gad

....

Joseph enters into a nearby Internet Suite on Level Eleven and decides to follow the advice given to him by the Innocent one.

Computer, Access 'Gods Great Computer' World Wide Web, Triple Six Dot Com …Logging On,

Joe

…Hi Gad, this is Joseph Blake online, an innocent told me how to find you here, so I was wondering if you could tell me whass up with everyone in Stereotypical?

Just then Joseph receives a reply.

Gad

...Aha I see that you got pass the initial assessment Mr Blake esquire, ha ha' finally its' you, and welcome to Gods great computer

Joe

Who are you, what do you want with me

Gad

...Fie Fi Fo Fum, the Devil himself wants to ask such inquisitive questions

Joe

...I'm not the bloody Devil

Gad

...Now, now, no need to get excited, I don't make the rules, now just for once play the game and let's assume that you are, now you don't have to like it but it would be easier if you accepted it and tried to enjoy it, that way you get to keep an edge on things

Joe

...You wanna give me advice, you try being in my shoes

Gad

...Only if they're a size 7 Joe, only if their a size 7

Joe

...So what am I suppose to do go around deceiving the nation or something?

Gad

...I'm beginning to like you already, well your on the right track, now listen and listen good God's great computer has a list of challenges for you, you have already passed the first stage by accessing this code, the next challenge is to represent Generation 7 against any members of Generation 6 in the performance arena, now you have to be inventive because the guilty don't like being preached to and the innocent like to be inspired, so watch your mouth so I hope you have an imagination that can span the stars in the sky coz you'll need it and by the way Joseph Blake be prepared for anything, but we should meet before long, as there is much to discuss

....

Now meanwhile as Joseph is communicating by voice email with Gad, the Compare of the events proceedings has appeared upon a stage in the discourse and recitals room.

[LEVEL TEN]
The Arena- The Theatre
Including
-{Recitals & Discourse}
-{Poetry & Prose}

-{Characterisation & Improvisations}
-{Stand Up Comedy}
-{Acoustics & Piano}

··

Compare

Don't be fooled by my appearance at first I will appear to you as a beautiful angel and the next you will see me as a hideous creature of the night but remember, you will only see me as I am and that is if you can see me at all, I am not tainted nor am I an innocent but I am what I am and that is what you see standing before you this evening

Chris

Seth who was that man you were talking to earlier?

Seth

Never mind, it's not important

Chris

Wasn't that the same guy we met last year?

Seth

Look! Its' not important, leave it, we've got to find Joe

Chris

But you upset him, he could be anywhere

Seth

He knows where we'll be, I bet you I know where he is

Chris

But I thought you were gonna take a challenge

Seth

I am, just not right now

Chris

Can I take a challenge on your behalf?

Seth

Why, you're not an elective?

Chris

Yeah but I can make a statement on your behalf can't I?

Seth

No its' between me and…

Chris

You and who

Seth

Never mind, it's not that important

Chris

Well at least let me open the floor for you, oh c'mon please Seth, at least let spit some lyrics on your behalf, I would love to do some spoken word and

Seth

Alright but keep it short I'm giving Joe no chances

Chris

So it's' Joseph isn't it, so tell me why the sudden hate campaign against Joe, something's wrong isn't it, what is it Seth, c'mon tell me

Seth

Don't worry about it, stop asking me questions, just wait for me in the arena, I'm going to see if Joe's on the Twelfth level

•••

Finally Gad and Joseph meet in person.

Joe

Are you Gad?

Gad

I see you are a man without insight or foresight or understanding

Joe

What makes you say that?

Gad

Because you ask a question that you already know the answer too, of course I am Gad, who else could or should I be

Joe

Yeah but…

Gad

…No buts, if you knew where to find me, then surely you should know who I am

Joe

Yeah I guess so but…

Gad

…No buts, I am here to answer your questions and to advise you on the matter concerning the knowledge and the wisdom that you seek of the 12

Joe

Am I one of the 12?

Gad

Yes and no, now come on we don't have all night for that matter

Joe

Well what does that mean?

Gad

It depends on you and your ability to follow instructions

Joe

And what instructions are those, and what if I don't wanna follow it

Gad

Its' up to you whether you choose to accept what I am about to tell you but If you don't then it could jeopardise the future of the 12

Joe

The future of the 12, so it does concern me then, so tell me what am I one of things that they call a Back Angel, or is this something more sinister and like those sordid deals, that everyone seems to be not so happy or willing to talk about

Gad

It concerns all of us esquire Blake who are connected to it

Joe

Well what is it that I should or should not accept according to what you're telling me?

Gad

Show me your hand,

Gad begins to use the art and method of palmistry to read Joseph's palm.

Gad

I see your character denotes good fortune, here take this and hold it tightly

Joe

What is it?

Gad

This Medallion, well its' a topaz, now never mind

Joe

What do I do with it?

Gad

You must hold it and repeat these words that I am about to tell you, but firstly Joe you must understand that the accurate knowledge that you have inside of you will bring about this everlasting future I suppose, if I can put it that way, now please focus and pay attention carefully as it could be just as easy to make a mistake or to be tricked or deceived by the craftiness of Generation 6, and just as easily it may come down to a judgement of error if we overlook this simplicity inside of us, as this is what the 12 Houses represents, now let us for one moment say that you are in the bible and that the bible is also inside of you, and then let us say that you are in the world and that the world is inside of you, and then let us say that the world is inside this Dome and that this dome is in Stereotypical, and then further still let us say that we are stereotypes of our former selves inside of this dome, which does not exist unless we do, and then and only then can you know your true purpose Joseph

Joe

Which is what?

Gad

Well if my hypothesis is indeed correct, if indeed this device does or does not work, which is one of binary synergy, analogy, now pay attention, for it is not the soul but the spirit that is God, which upon in having within it the breath of life and nothing more, no attachments, no permutations, no plausibility, no eventuality, nothing at all whatsoever, just breath, so keep breathing, and just relax and breathe

Joe

Well I am

Gad

Now while you are busy breathing we must find the answer to all of these questions

Joe

But what questions?

Gad

The ones that the Digital Angel is seeking, now we must meditate on these simple teachings and pursue love with vigour along with the desire to acquire spiritual gifts so that when you address us in your presence, that you must especially speak for the edification of the 12 Houses

Gad leads Joseph up to the Cyber Synchronisation Suite on [LEVEL ELEVEN] The Suite / Internet Video & DVD Games-Interactive Suite, Cyber Synchronisation, and begins to straps and attaches him to a Cyber Synchronisation apparatus while Joseph is tightly clutching the Topaz, which is slowly releasing an hallucinogen into his bloodstream, in order for Gad to

attempt to initiate a prototype procedure known to Generation 7 as Transhalucigenicstate.

••

[LEVEL TWELVE]
The HOUSES

At the point in time, Angel Ruen has made his way up to level Twelve and has locate the whereabouts of Obadiah 144, and as their eyes meet for the first time, for a moment silent falls upon the lips of the now fearful and trembling Obadiah.

Obadiah 144

I've been expecting you Black Angel

Angel Ruen

Then there is no need for me to tell you why I am here

Obadiah 144

Are you the one my prince, as it was prophesied a long time ago that there would come an Angel of Mercy when the presence of God would cease to move over the Earth, which some would say was the beginning of this unpredictable age

Angel Ruen

Yes I am aware of this time age old prophecy, as it was a time when the Ophanim upon the throne of God did interactively cease to account for the multitudes of Man and Woman alike, but at that time

I slept, as I was preferred rather dead to the world at large, although I myself could have foreseen and predicted this age of which you are now subject too, as back then the world was already at an end

Obadiah 144

Then tell me my Angel, are you the Angel of Darkness or an Angel Of Light, or are you the one permitted to end all things, or to begin all things, as I see that you wield the sword of truth, or can you tell me what else is to become of us and this newly born infant child of our time, if we are all seemingly destined to perish by your Will

Angel Ruen

Nay, nay Obadiah do not fear me, for I am only the beacon of death

Obadiah 144

So you are a Sign, an Omen, an Omega

Angel Ruen

Perhaps, yes I am, but you will be saved by this sword of truth, except that you will not be saved by me or within a way that you could imagine

Obadiah 144

Then by what cause Dark Angel shall we be saved

Angel Ruen looks around and about himself somewhat disappointed with his surroundings.

Angel Ruen

Back then things were so much easier, as he so loved Mankind in embracing his to his bosom, but now that we once again have the upper hand, it would seem that it is you who has fallen out of favour with him

Obadiah 144

Well I have always kept and maintained a record of the Dome\s events ever since my learned years have enabled me too, albeit events of unusual activity

Angel Ruen

Events! Events, what do you know of events, this record of Man's history is nothing but useless idol baseless mongering, but this child that you speak of, is he a Messiah or not

Obadiah 144

No my Angel, I'm afraid to say it, but the child is not, except that...

Angel Ruen

Except that what Obadiah?

Obadiah 144

I Was going to say except that He is actually a She, and so therefore no not a Messiah as you so put it, although somewhat Angelic, like you I suppose, in that yes for a long time ever since we have held our beliefs that a saviour could be born, but it seems that we have led ourselves astray, but she bears all the qualities and fortunes of being completely and purely Human if you like

Angel Ruen

Another Earth Mother perhaps, yes I understand it now, except these records that you have made Obadiah 144 are of no use or consequence to me, or for anyone for that fact, for what you have summonsed in me is irreversible, for what is about to take place will leave no trace of Mankind's face upon the face of it, for when I go to your fathers' house, you shall know then why I have come and why Will, shall be done

Obadiah 144

Please my Prince, have mercy and show us good faith, for we did not know what we were doing in the absences of God

Angel Ruen

Once the child is in my possession, you shall have your mercy as you have requested it.

Obadiah 144

But I cannot, for I now fear for her safety

Angel Ruen

Do not tempt me Obadiah, for I could destroy this entire unsavoury and unholy place in an instant

Obadiah 144

So you do intend to kill her?

Just then Angel Ruen became furious.

Angel Ruen

Now listen to me you prophet of doom, for it is you and your kind that has called upon God's creatures to answer your call and to do your bidding, and yet whenever your prophetic judgments are not fulfilled or come into any fruition, then you have the arrogant audacity to think that your Will is superior to all, and yet when things do not suit you, and when things do not go your way you pray to God to command the Heaven's to fulfil your plea and bargaining, now I'll ask you one more time, give me the child or I will decapitate and behead where you stand.

Obadiah 144

Please my Black Angel, Believe me my prince, I shall do your bidding, except that first we must wait a short time, and then I shall do your bidding, for I am not exactly sure where the child is right now or what has become of her

Angel Ruen

Very well then Obadiah as you say, but remember Prophet, that time is of no consequence to me, for you shall pay either way

Just then Agent Rumsfold, Tork of Naphtali and Sethaniel Newton have met up secretly, having been plotting something sinister and auspicious all along concerning the 12 Houses.

Agent Rumsfold

Where have you been, I've been waiting for you to carry out my instruction

Seth

I had to get rid of Christine, why where is he

Tork of Naphtali

You can find him in Cyber Synchronisation suite, he's with Gad of the Sagittarians, form the Seventh house

Seth

I know but what shall I do, he's not so easily deceived

Agent Rumsfold

Offer him a deal, if he accepts it then I'll take it from there but if not you'll have to do as we planned, no doubt Gad is going to cause a bit of a problem,

Tork of Naphtali

Like what?

Agent Rumsfold

Like if he converts Joseph Blake, I want you to kill him personally

Seth

Are you serious, kill who Joe?

Agent Rumsfold

Yes, now take this gun and don't miss or you'll have me to answer too, I'll give you the signal when, I'll be watching and waiting

Tork of Naphtali

I cannot do this act Rumsfold, for there is not profit in deceit, I beg you let Seth do it

Agent Rumsfold

Do it or face the consequences Tork, as you know this Mark carries a lot of weight behind it, and this is the only place where the freedom of expression is permitted, Blake's number could change all that, if he complies with the new regulations being proposed by the eighth house and Generation 6 will have little or no influence in the running of future Generations

Seth

Yes I know but killing him, you said there would be no killing, its' against all the Houses

Agent Rumsfold

If they want to pursue the will of a Prophecy, then they must pay the consequences, so far all proposed activities have been abandoned from any input or resources from Generation 6, in the beginning the houses couldn't function without us, this new legislation has been transmitted freely without any engagement with our approval or input of practical guidelines, its' a threat to us all, I want full power and autonomy over the Digital Program

Seth

You want me to murder and execute an innocent all because of your stupid rules and regulations, for this so called secrecy act, that's absurd, it s evil, I won't, I won't do it

Agent Rumsfold

If we can control the electives, then surely Blake and Gad are no match for the intelligence behind our systems, you know you could also profit in the future from this venture Seth, otherwise I'll destroy you and your career, now he must be taken down or else, now you've both been warned

Just then Christina approaches the Compare upon the stage and is invited to address the unsuspecting crowd.

....

Compare

I would like to say that it is a great and wonderful experience to be here tonight and I would like to propose a toast in good faith to

everyone here who came to see in the New Year and celebrate the month of Capricorn with Tork from the House of Napthali, so cheers, now I would like to welcome to the stereotypical stage without further ado, a new face and hopefully a new influential talent and commodity from the house of Reuben the Taurus and speaking on behalf of Generation 6, 'Christina Scott'

The Crowd

Boo, boo, blasphemer, heretic, boo

Chris

I would just like to start by saying, that some of us dream the dream and some of us create the dream, we build it from the ideology and vision of our hearts minds until it becomes a reality, some of us use this reality in order to make it a better world although that is not entirely everyone's dream, but we would like to think so, because the dream is for everyone and although I am in my 2nd year of maturity I have already gained the skills to access future pathways in order to achieve a higher state of being

A Tainted

She doesn't speak like us, who is she?

Chris

As my thought processes takes me from dream to dream, and what is necessary to fulfil my ultimate goal and purpose in this wretched life is left up to me to motivate myself up to my highest potential, which when at its' highest peak allows my dream to flourish and reach its' point of success, this happens by engaging with other dreamers of the Generations, anyway I hope it will become clear in time, I know I have never been philosophical up until now, but you and I are in a constant state of growth and development so the best thing is to trust your instincts, am I right, or am I right

....

Just then Sethaniel and Gad and Tork, enter [LEVEL ELEVEN] of the Interactive Suite, as Gad disconnects Joe from the Cyber Synchronisation apparatus.

Seth

Ya know Joe you have this amazing ability to speak the truth as if everything were so easy, straightforward and simple, well its' not is it, so tell me my good man, do you really believe that any one gives a dam about anything that you have to say?

Joe

Well…

Seth

…Well exactly, they don't, they don't Joe coz no one cares, and no one gives a dam about you or anyone so…

Joe

…So why are you wasting your time telling me all this?

Seth

Look Joe, I think you know I didn't come here to spit words in your face, but its' over Joe, so you can stop the bullshit because there is no seventh heaven, it all ends here with you and me, I thought you would have seen the light by now, I tried to turn you around gently but you were stubborn, I thought you were a challenge

Joe

That's your problem Seth, you think it's' all a game

Seth

Don't tell me you couldn't see it coming Joe, I didn't wanna break your spirit, you're a nice guy Joe, I thought you were a star but you're so dumb, I just don't know why I even bothered with you

Joe

Well why are you bothering now?

Seth

Because I've come to offer you a chance to redeem yourself and make good out of all this misunderstanding

Joe

What do you know about good intentions?

Seth

Alright, I'm sorry, I'm sorry, I didn't mean to offend you, its' just that sometimes you piss me off, you always think about yourself, when there's others to consider, people who matter and they're just as important as you like Christina and me for instance

Joe

Yeah right, well where's Christina now, no doubt your keeping the truth from her as well, well I'm sorry too, but I don't know why, or what I was thinking, you're really something Seth, and you have the balls to call me screwed up

Seth

Don't you know we love you, we care about you, but you're always getting the wrong end of the stick, were here for you, me and Chris, just believe that, and its' alright, c'mon Joe lets go have a good time and forget this

Just then Agent Rumsfold makes an appearance and a gesture towards Sethaniel.

Joe

Who's ya friend Seth?

Seth

Oh he's just a dear old friend Joe, yuh know, just a mate, surely yuh know most of all, that we all need friends in this life, yuh know to get ahead

140

Agent Rumsfold

My name is Rumsfold, it's always a pleasure to meet a good friend of Seth's

Joe

Rumsfold, that sounds familiar, have we met before?

Seth

No you've never met him before, its' quite impossible

Joe

He's an agent isn't he, he's Generation 6,
I know it, he is, isn't he Seth?

Seth

No its' not true

Agent Rumsfold

Its' too late Seth, he knows

Seth

Alright he is, but before you make up your mind tell him what's going on

Joe

I already know

Seth

But do you Joe, you don't, its' not what it seems, you're a product, just like the rest of us

Joe

What do you mean I'm a product, a product of what?

Agent Rumsfold

The product of a company

Joe

That's absurd, what the hell are you talking about, tell me who I am

Agent Rumsfold

You are who you say you are, but the rest is fabrication you are the creation of a company called the Digital Chip Corporation, a company who uses bio-tech medicines combined with Implanting, In Vitro Fertilisation under laboratory conditions, they took various cells for D.N.A testing and then you were cloned and reproduced, the chip which you wear in your left hand carries all the data we need to know all about you Joseph Blake

Joe

No that's not true, you're lying

Seth

Then tell us the truth

Agent Rumsfold

No Joe you are the liar, you never had a mother or a father because you were created

Joe

No its' not true, why don't you believe me

Agent Rumsfold

Its' not about what I believe, its' the truth

Joe

You think I'm messed up

Agent Rumsfold

No, but you are a devil's disciple aren't you Joe

Joe

No way Man! What do you mean?

Agent Rumsfold

Why don't you ask Gad

Joe

Gad is it true?

Gad

Yes and no, not exactly, your just different from the rest of us, only a Devil in disguise would try to project his appearance and persona onto a potential innocent victim, whilst similarly presenting himself as truth

Joe

Just tell me the truth Gad and stop messing me around

Gad

Not before they leave, they're presence here is jeopardising everything, I must speak with you alone Joe and in confidence, now if you don't mind gentlemen as you can see were busy, so we can take up this matter up later or if you want to challenge Joe, we will be in the arena before midnight

••

Meanwhile in the Arena, Christian is being booed off stage

The Crowd

Boo, boo, get her off

Joe

What's that?

Gad

That's the crowd in the arena, someone is performing, look Joe it is imperative that you understand the 12 Houses because if you don't you will build up resistance, which will in turn result in negative action, and the system doesn't accept reactionaries not now, not ever, it could displace your role in future progressions of your placement in the shape of everything that we've built up, I know that I'm not the person that you want to hear this from, and I accept your phobias and fears but it does not matter, your role has already been defined and chosen, If you wish to have a life partner then it doesn't' matter to the system if they are male or female nor does it matter whatever colour, country or background they are from as long as they dwell in the same House as you then it is acceptable to the system, this is the only ruling division you must comply with, even if I had a child, if the child were born or cloned of me if it did not carry the same sign of my house then it would be removed and nurtured and then eventually it would grow and make progress according to the teachings of that House and not my own as once ordained

Joe

So I am a clone

Gad

No, No quite the opposite, your quite unique, now try not to worry about it, you have the key to freedom if you so choose it, this is only the beginning of your initiation when it is complete then your life will truly begin

Joe

So why are Rumsfold and Seth trying to bring me down?

Gad

It was your father who started Generation 6, then the corporation with a new CEO, took over and started manipulating Digital Angels Access Codes to re-direct more electives into their households without going through the representative bodies, this is illegal and is also know as a Black Angel, once the codes are changed they can't be checked or matched against any previously recorded numbers given to the students, and so we in Generation 7 did develop a prototype to try and recognise Black Angels but it couldn't calculate the numbers unless they were in sequence with the 12 Houses, the numbers used by Generation 6 were random up until they used the number of man which is Six, Six, Six, that's the number assigned to you I believe, so there must be some deep underlying reason why they chose to use this number on you, I do believe that you must pose a threat of a most significant and important nature to their

House, so I must ask you now to trust me until I can consult with Obadiah 144, and the senior masters of the houses and the elders

· · · · · · · · · · ·.............· ·

Christina Scott is now on stage reciting a poem to the unsuspecting audience.

Chris

Who broke the ring of eternity, who divorced themselves from life, who experiments with the act of procreation, who sacrifices breath for suffocation, whose breast does not feed mankind, monolistically I am the iron maiden a ship that sails the tide, stereotypically I am just a woman with a girl that lives inside, who's femininity knows no graces, whose mother is eternally damned, who's virginity is chastened by torment who's eve to behold Mary's hand, who's love us left us mourning never loving any man, monolistically I am the iron maiden a ship that sails the tide, stereotypically I am just a woman with a girl that lives inside, who's judgement is the harlot great whose abominations are a sacred fate, whose perdition is Babylon's fall, who will answer when I call, who knows the story of one and all, monolistically I am the iron maiden a ship that sails the tide, stereotypically I am just a woman with a girl that lives inside

Agent Rumsfold

It would seem that Gad has alternative plans for Mr Blake, but we must not allow him to win any converts in the arena, it could result in something more detrimental to our house, you must make a mockery and a laughing stock of him in the arena, no doubt if he is perceived as an incompetent then no one will take them seriously

147

Tork of Napthali

It should be quite easy to ridicule Joseph Blake, he's quite the romantic with foolish idea's about the concepts of life, I should impress upon the Tainted nature of life to win over any sceptical or undecided opinions of Generation 6

Agent Rumsfold

Good!

....

Joseph and Gad arrive on [LEVEL TWELVE] The HOUSES Where Obadiah 144 and Angel Ruen are waiting.

Gad

I'm afraid the infrastructure of the 12 Houses is breaking down into separate interpretations of what the basic teachings and the code of practice should be, especially for the senior members, I believe that Tork of Naphtali may have led us astray

Obadiah 144

Well Gad, although the present ordinances still influence everyday life the 12 Houses still maintain their links with its' senior members and the elders, we have been observing Tork of Naphtali closely for quite some time as being the main developing source of this rift between the houses

Gad

Yes but what is alarmingly disturbing, is the attitude of Generation 6 towards the values and the relationship between us, as we are now only beginning to challenge the changing role of subjects on conceptual race and gender, if the senior members of the houses set out and define what is an acceptable view that we should all adopt, whether it be acceptance, forgiveness, tolerance or understanding, then surely all the other Houses should follow suit and comply with this as being the acceptable norm and balance of all things

Angel Ruen

I think the defining example is set out in 'Mathew 7 versus 1 and 2, where it states, "Judge not that you be not judge, for with what judgment you judge you will be judged; and with the measure you use, it will be measured back to you

Gad

You mean the 12 houses

Angel Ruen

It all depends upon who is the judge, and who is making the judgement, and who is to be judged

Obadiah 144

Yes but we can make no decisive Judgement or take any action at this present time, although some persons have tried to perpetrate the purpose of this organisation and bring the Houses into disrepute, I think the nature of the source is not to look too closely at what Tork of Naphtali and Generation 6 are up to, but for you to help find the Child and locate the messenger, as I believe, no in fact I am sure that she may have been the last and only link that contained any traces of Human DNA in his Genome mapping, to ably and productively reproduce this child

Joe

Then the messenger was Mary

Obadiah 144

Was she one, with whom you met Joseph?

Joe

Yes, it was Mary Hampden

Gad

But what can be done, for without the application of using 'transhalucigenicstate, which as you know isn't quite ready, but if this is true, then Humanity can become reborn, but is it sustainable, can it be supported by this current climate

Obadiah 144

Yes but we've never had a black angel before, and as no other clone can reproduce, then we must assume that her mapping was also known by other members of the Elected Houses

Gad

I thought you might have considered that option, but it could result in a negative outcome, surely this kind of control has leaked down into our personal lives far too much, I mean the power of the church is a direct conflict of interest within the governing bodies and the application of ethics and morals which are also of a poor and low standard

Obadiah 144

It is up to you and your house to organise and vote in an order that promotes conscientious stability and accountability and transparency, of course we need clones for productivity, but bio technology has changed the way we live, and work and organise ourselves, more than at other time in our history, we have cloned Humankind in the vain hope of sustaining and maintain the reigns of rigid structuring for political gain, and these clones were designed for specific roles and duties, in the early nineties society established this social order and developed this police state we have now come to embrace, and in order to keep control on crime, the wheels of life are now turning against us, everything must be constructed for a specific task and role in this advancing democracy

Gad

You speak of visions 144, but my only concern is of the members of my House, as you know Generation 7 have been much of a redundant and inactive force since Generation 6 have been trying to take control of all the Houses

Obadiah 144

Yes I am aware of the activities of Generation 6, but still so it should
be a fair electoral process, but this bio-tech revolution has made
influential power change hands more and more corruptly, and there
is now this newly elected parliamentary rule that has requested
that everything and everyone is set up to a programme under the
conditions of the Generations, and subject through the Houses to
meet with the ruling bodies, this is the formula which we must now
use and adopt as our own, each one of us must address the task
of his or her intended role, but I suppose if a pure Human already
existed, then that would inevitably change everything, and it could
also signify the end of current system, making it ineffective and
redundant, it would also be the fulfilment of a prophecy that none
had thought possible until now

Gad

But the boy, he is only a 1st year

Obadiah 144

Yes, but on the subject of Joseph Blake, if you can persuade him
to address the subject of faith and belief, then does not sex, colour
and race disappear from view, then the real stem of truth surely
comes upon us, as one body, if we are all indeed glorified, as I do
not say these things lightly, but it is the saving grace that brings us
salvation through the word and I dearly bid you not to set yourselves
up against one another, because if you find indifference with one
another, then it is better to believe and understand that the 12 Houses
and their values extend to every one of us by faith, you must proceed

with caution and process the boy but keep it clean, or you'll have me to answer to

Gad

Thank you 144

Joe

So tell me Gad what else were you keeping from me, or are you part of this conspiracy?

Gad

Its' no conspiracy Joe

Joe

So why the secrets, I thought I could trust you but this is so unbelievable, so who or what is the Digital Chip Corporation, and who dreamt up what seems to be the worst nightmare of my life, and you can cut the bullshit about Generation 6, because right now because I don't believe you, or anything, or anyone

Gad

Well like it or not Joe, you're going to have to believe me, or you can follow your so called friends, because what you don't know is that Tork of Napthali has let loose a hindrance in his ambitions to gain influential dealings with Generation 6 and this has put the 12 Houses in an unstable position, what with these forthcoming elections

Joe

So how does all this tie in with me, what's going on Gad?

Gad

The Digital Chip Corporation maintains a partnership with the Generations but what I neglected to tell you, is that the stone I gave to you contains a very potent and valuable property which allows the user to experience a very enlightening configuration which will induce a very surreal and supernatural phenomenon, you may as well know that even as we speak the topaz is releasing a small dose of an hallucinogen into your blood stream, which is otherwise referred to as transhalucigenistate, now we must return to the Cyber Synchronisation suite to complete the full sequence

Joe

You did what?

Gad

Listen Joe, we have learnt that your number 1.4.7 translates into 7.7.7 which is why you were the ideal target to bring the 12 houses into disrepute, you carry the perfect arrangement for a number of sequences that may reveal why you are and who you are, and you will also notice that my Digi Chip is placed in my right hand while yours is in your left hand, obviously you were mapped or created to bring balance to the Houses and I think that Generation 6 also know this, which is why they chose you as their victim

154

Joe

So what does this trans symmetry state thing do, what's gonna happen to me Gad?

Gad

It will help you to relate to the laws of life, transhalucigenicstate is a level of consciousness whereby the mind is suspended in an animated system of time projected through a stasis, the stasis is a kind of system where recorded events of the mind are relative to their actual intended time, this experience is believed to be a passage through to higher consciousness where you will be contained momentarily in the stasis, it will tutor your every thought and emotion

Joe

But what do I do in the stasis, I don't like anyone playing with my mind Gad, seriously man its' no joke

Gad

I will not play with your mind Joe, but it was up to us Generation 7 to uphold and protect the current issues on legislation for cloning and the natural environment, because cloning is becoming more and more dangerous to the development of our race and species, which could also proved to be damaging to our natural ability to grow and develop, and it could be that you are the last link to what it is to be pure Human, as through human beings, transhalugicgenicstate works in total opposition to these cancerous cells and defects that we find

155

in clones, that stop and disable us from reproducing naturally, but I must tell you that it does also induce auditory hallucinations, that is why everything that you now know had to be assimilated through cyber synchronisation

Joe

You mean I'm gonna start tripping any minute right

Gad

Yes, but I will talk you through it, now
please remain calm and be ready

Joe

Ok I'm ready

[LEVEL ELEVEN] Gad attaches Joseph to the Cyber Synchronization apparatus and begins to activate the apparatus Transhalucigenicstate, The Cyber Synchronization Suite is an interactive registry program, that contains a digital databank of all the students that are logged and recorded as active members across the Dome International, it is a Databank, where students can be paired up evenly and equally matched with a respective partner from the same House, although initially and formally these Generations must be of the same grouping worldwide, as it was by now left to Gad to manipulate the Digital Sequence that would reconfigure this database, in order for Joseph to navigate beyond these predetermined codes, and to go outside of the normal registration of his own House, in order to find and

become realigned and allied to Mary, of whom they believed was the real DNA messenger.

Gad

Because Generation 6 were not completely satisfied with our ruling on clones they wish to find a way to end or delete the current program or rules of existence, as they are also set on creating a Digital world which is automated as well as computerised, this is why we have Digital chips in our hands, but we had some influence on the implementation of this device, Generation 6 is also the reason why there is an imbalance in the 12 Houses, but they cannot function without us, nor us without them but that could all change at any time, as both parties have presented their own blue prints on how to achieve self sufficient independence from the reliance of one House to another house, but this cannot easily be done or achieved in a healthy and practical way without destabilising the environment unless we can achieve a balanced break or divide between all the Houses from One to Twelve, so you can see this has resulted in a unhappy compromise where we are now part digital and part clone, and less able to maintain ourselves in a natural environment, so now there is a bitter rift between us

Joe

So what you're saying now is that I'm more human that clone, but if we're all clones,

Joseph begins to enter into a hypnotic trance whilst attempting to maintain a logical level of communication with Gad.

157

Joe

Hey Gad, ha ha, that's really funny man

Gad

Now Joe, its' beginning, and no not all of us are clones, just some of us, now I'm gonna access some codes, which will rotate a sequence and integrate you into the Cybernetic Genesis, this should reveal all of your Digital Cybernetic Code.

[ACCESSING...1 2 3 4 5 6 7 14 21 28
35 42 49 56 63 70 77 84 91 98]

Just then Gad starts talking to himself.

The cleansing and the exposing of the soul revealeth everything in the third eye that can now see, now for this potent medicinal properties, that I might hasten to add to this medallion, which has given over the answer to the truth in all completeness, except that for the last few days are also the first rays of sunlight now beckoning, as I now know what is possible and what is not to be done, and also what I must do, but is it possible for the spirit and not the soul as previously thought, to cross over and transcend into the subconscious dimension leaving the physical plain, and as I am aware that the spirit is eternal but the body is not, but be aware Joe, that we are all running out of time and without knowing who or where the messenger is in Dome Europe, then it is hard to explore all the other possibilities, but all these signs seem to indicate that your that number 6.6.6. is rectified to its original sequence, that is 1.4.7

is sequenced, then perhaps the equivalence should automatically appear.

...CODE TRANSLATING...
[98 91 84 77 70 63 56 49 42 35 28 21 14 7 6 5 4 3 2 1]

[...MESSENGER MARY HAMPDEN...]

DIGITAL ACCESS CODE COMPUTING,..... INTEL NO. 258
AFFRIMATIVE...HAMPDEN MARY

Just then something strangely profound and metaphysically began to take effect, as Joseph's mind seem to fall into darkness, until it began to race and speed along through a tunnel of what appeared to be a rapid succession of vaguely enhanced and obscurely unfolding events, that instantly resulted with Joseph finding himself becoming transported into what seemed and felt like a lucid dream, as this Digital process had allowed for Joseph to communicate through his mind's response directly with Mary.

....

And so it was that all of the winged Angels of the Empyreans and some of which who were not winged, did appear to Mankind across the entirety of the Globe, which was the Dome and the Domain of the Dominions, awaiting to hear and to then Sing out their cries of finite seconds, when all that ever was would cease to be.

....

Joe

The messenger, who's the messenger?

Gad

I was hoping you could tell me that, surely Mary was in the system before I became a programmer, as your number is the most accurate match for a predestined set of coordinates, then there must be a recipient number of what or who we call a messenger initiator

Joe

Wow! I feel great, its' so impossible to tell whether time is speeding up or slowing down, I mean even when we look at mans inventions of time it is an inaccurate device for measuring time clocks go back in winter and forward is summer, Is that what you discovered when you tried to explore the Tran symmetry continuum

Gad

That's right Joe, good your connected, it is proving to be effective in our research as were moving away from the centre of our life force, hence" our ability and need to keep changing and adapting to our environment

Joe

Gad I'm learning at such a rapid rate that it is almost impossible to know whether we are really within our own material existence by reason or definition, my interpretation is that if we slowdown our resistance, like falling asleep while on a fast moving train then we begin to see glimpses of the parallel sub conscious appearing intermittently at every glance, but now I see that the intervals are becoming more and more sustainable

Gad

Joe don't fall asleep, its' imperative that you stay awake, do not fall asleep we need you to locate the messenger initiator, and the je ne sais quoi, as they say in Dome France

Just then something strangely profound and metaphysically began to take effect on Joseph senses, as this Digital process had allowed for Joseph to communicate through his Mind's response directly with Mary Hampden.

Joe

Mary start again...

Mary

Is it true did they tell you?

Joe

Yes, yes they did

Mary

I have a child Joe, she's human,

Joe

But why didn't you tell me before

Mary

Because I couldn't', they wouldn't let me, the Houses in knowing how you felt about things, wouldn't have agreed to it

Joe

But Mary, I wanted to be with you, tell me now where is the child,

Mary

I don't know but its' all for the greater good of the Generations Joe, but if there's one thing I can tell you is that I love you, and you can be sure that for us to be together, then you must put our numbers together Joe, now be a man of heart, bye Joe, bye…

Joe

No! Mary but wait, we need to know what House she is in, it was you, you were the messenger, it was you all along…

[...TRANSLATION COMPLETE …]

Just then Joseph becomes consciously ware of his surroundings, as he wakes up out of his lucid dream.

Joe

Gad..?

Gad

Tell me Joseph, what did you see Joe?

Joe

I saw Mary

Gad

Where was she?

Joe

Its' hard to believe that you can be in a room and still go anywhere, places, many, many places, she was saying something, she was right here

Gad

What was she doing?

Joe

I don't know, I couldn't distinguish that

Gad

Was it the messenger, was there any message?

Joe

I'm not sure, something about a man of heart, to put the numbers together

Gad

A man of heart, what did she mean, put the numbers together, what numbers Joe, think boy think

Joe

It was Mary, she was right here I tell you, and the child, the child was mine but I wasn't there and She was, it was Mary, someone who I had touched and felt, and now they've taken her away from me, but why Gad, why, how can we have a Child and never really know the consequence of our actions, I couldn't even feel or touch or get to know her

Gad

I am saddened by your loss and regret Joe, but at least it means everything is well, you've done well to explain the vision and because you are of the 7th house the woman and child will be taken care of in theirs, I will inform Obadiah 144 of this eventual enlightenment but the time is not now, nor do we have all things that we need for time to come to pass but you have proved that transhalucigenicstate works and we must enlist future minds to engage with us upon this amazing discovery

Joe

Amazing is that what you call it, all you seem to be concerned about is messages,, when your tampering still may be flawed Gad, who's to say that what I felt or heard was even real, when it could just be a dream or even hallucinations, what makes you so sure it was this methodology, that you drugged me to get you desired effect

Gad

Everything that happened to you before, happened for a reason right up to the point until we met, I am simply here to help you through all the stages of your initiation into this House, everything I told you was the truth, not your truth, not my truth, but the eternal truth, everything you witnessed since gaining access to transhalucigenicstate has now been logged and recorded for the purpose of the 12 Houses, this is how we prepare and organise ourselves according to new data and information for future Generations, the technique also proves that this directly works positively against the defective gene which we inherited from cloning by stimulating the nerve receptors which carry the messages to and from the brain, I think now is the time to present ourselves to the others in the arena, although it may take a while for you to recover

....

The Master of Ceremonies, the elected Compare, invite Sethaniel Newton onto the stage to address the on looking crowd.

Compare

And now without further delay we have the event of the night, all that you have been waiting for, as many of you are already familiar with the notoriety of Sethaniel Newton, a man of great productivity and firmly fixed in character, a man's who depreciation of the Generations is infamously known throughout, and might I hasten to add an elected member from the house of Benjamin the Aries

Crowd

We want Benjamin, We want Benjamin, We want Benjamin the Ram, Yeah!

Just then Joseph and Gad enter the arena and approach the stage.

Compare

But wait, wait for it, we have a challenger, a man of fear and servility, a man who's ubiquity has come before us, And they seek him here and they seek him there and they seek him almost everywhere and now they have found him, what they are looking for from the House of Gad the Sagittarian, we have Joseph Blake, the innocent explorer, so now without further ado, let the soothsaying soliquay commence

Crowd

Hooray! Boo, boo, hooray

Joe

Once upon a time there was nothing and nothing went about the vast space turning anything in its' path into nothing until one fateful day

there was nothing left, and when nothing had seen what he had done he became sad and sorrowful as an empty vacuum stood before him, so he prayed and prayed until one day his prayer was answered and nothing begot everything, and so now when we look around, everything is where nothing was

Crowd

Bullshit! Rubbish,

A Tainted

Who the hell is this guy, get him off, he's nuts, Seth's gonna cane and crucify him

An Innocent

Very passive, but interesting, but what is he leading up to, where is he going with all this?

Seth

Even if you died today Joe, you would be none the wiser about God or any other faith you profess, because the funny thing is you are nothing and your right there is nothing beyond this world, the only thing is that an idiot like you can't see that, you can say whatever you want and it doesn't matter not to me, not to you, not to anyone, God could be a democratically elected communist for all we care but it amounts to nothing, nothing at all

A Tainted

Go on Seth! Tell him, and tell him again, he's no good, he thinks he better than the rest of us, well he ain't, he's no good

Joe

You know Seth, I always ask myself why do piss takers always accuse everyone of taking themselves too seriously, and you know I figured out that maybe it's' because they can't take themselves seriously

Crowd

Bring on Seth, Bring on Seth, Bring on Seth

Seth

I am not afraid of you thou you say life may bear no peace, a construction of the beautiful with bitter wine your skin beneath, a deception of the cunning was not beauty beside beast, I know you not as master in the house that you dwell thou you often speak of heaven and damn my life to hell, an idea of believers which people are deceived, present me with no bible for I do not care to read, liar, liar, liar now where oh where to run, I hear you speak of kingdoms but I do not see them come, I'm not afraid of you thou I often hear your name, you say love may have no equal, but you do not know my game, liar, liar, liar its' you I should accuse, so fear me God almighty for the time has come to choose, I'll haunt you by the graveside and taunt you while you sleep, I'll shake the heavens gateway, while serpents strike you deep, liar, liar, liar you call yourself a son, so as it is written

so let it be done, you make me beg for mercy, which love has not no shame, I accept responsibly, but you're the one to blame, liar, liar, liar appeasing to no truth, the whole world burns aflame but they still do not know you, condemn me to damnation with words that can't be seen from 1066 to 1914, a thousand years of fury, which hell cannot be found you wish that the abyss
is where I should be bound

The Crowd react with mixed responses.

Crowd

Boo, boo, Yeah, yeah, blasphemy, heresy, yeah, boo, boo

Joe

Wait a minute, you planned this, you set
this up, everything here is a test

Seth

Very good Joe, you understand very much, very too
late to change the outcome, and what can you do to help
yourself there isn't a thing that you can do or say that
I can't counteract, I control everything here Joe

Joe

Well if that were true there would be no need for you to toy with me
in such a way, maybe I don't understand the rules of the game but I
won't be your pawn

169

Seth

Then kill yourself, here I'll give you the opportunity to do it

Joe

Kill myself, and what, what will that benefit the innocents here tonight, I am here on behalf of their truth, and I know deep down that your more afraid of me now than the truth itself

Seth

Look you may well have the answer but you do not know the question and that my friend is where you'll lose, you speak of fear of the unknown but you do not recognise a single shred of your own imaginings, you and your kind created this place out of your own denials, this place is purgatory and I am its' keeper, and only I can determine the outcome of what takes place here tonight

Joe

Seth I already know the answer to my question, but the thing is that you don't, as the games that you play are heartless, and Rumsfold is pulling all the puppet strings, so I let me say to you now, that even if I lose here tonight, then you must do the right thing, whatever happens, and Generation 6 must yield any influence it may have over the other houses, is that a deal?

Agent Rumsfold

With what leverage does he asks for so much

Seth

He cannot know the answer, let him have his bargain, if he is wrong then the other houses will yield to us, do you agree Joseph?

Joe

Yes I agree

Compare

Begin

Joe

The question is what is the most important thing in the zodiac, therefore the answer is the stars and the constellations which are influenced in us, and what you see before you today is its' earthly manifestation, the 12 houses which are completely reliant on the continual movement of energy and intellectual wisdom both nurturing and naturally evolving into the system that you see before you today and that is the answer to the question, but if a Human being existed today, then that would contradict and undo everything as we now know it, the emotional scars, the symptoms of carrying the weight of the struggle, the anguish of torment, the burdens upon the souls sacrifice, the trials of life, the pains of time, we are all here and we have all been tested beyond the limits of our endeavors, we have tried to love, and we have tried to fulfill an unspoken human contract to one another, at times we have failed and yet we try and try again, through the mire and toxicity of unrequited affections, the loss of touching with the simplest and truest of intentions, with the gravity of the world bearing down upon us, along with the personal conviction of facing another day, the reality of guilt, realizing, that we must forgive each other, and that we must rise above this dichotomy, and that we must aim or even choose to be wise with our words, and to love in as many ways, If we were once the babies of children, who became as adolescent teenagers, and now young adults, who go on to become Men and Women, wish in our ways to learn and to live and to love and to embrace this world of our creation, in becoming contented in our old age, accepting as individuals, our faults and imperfections, growing gracefully towards our satisfaction of peace and contentment, if only to see that life is circle of family, friends, acquaintances, companions and lovers, who only choose upon deciding to love us unconditionally, as we are, as we once were, as what we will be, then surely we can do the same, so choose your path carefully.

Just then everyone looks puzzled and confused.

Seth

Is that the answer?

Agent Rumsfold

Mr Newton, Kill him, do it now

Sethaniel Newton pulls out the Gun he was concealing and takes aim and fires at Joseph, but just as Gad see's this event unfolding and pushes Joseph to one side and falls into the line of fire.

Gad

Stop! Wait! Joseph watch out, No!

Gad is struck by the straying bullet and falls to the ground.

Joe

You've killed him

Sethaniel panics and attempts to flee the scene, but is stopped in his tracks by some of the crowd.

Seth

No! I didn't mean it, it wasn't' suppose to end like this

Joe

Gad can you hear me? Gad say something, Gad…

Gad

I'm alright, I'm ok, its' only a flesh wound, I'll survive, now that they've finally played their last hand, now speak to the people Joe and remember…you're a man of heart, you're a man of heart Joe, as I know what Mary meant when she said put the Digital numbers together to uncover where the Child is.

Joseph looks around at the crowd, who watch him cautiously and with an air of suspense and anticipative silence.

Joe

Once upon a time many, many moons ago in a far off land there lived a man o' heart, now this man o' heart he was a good man he was, and he was loved by all the people in the land. Now one day the man o' heart was out walking when he comes across these chickadees, beautiful these chickadees was and the man o' heart was overcome by his senses because he did not know nor never seen such beautiful chickadees like these. Now the man o' heart was a caring and loving man and he was concerned about a lot of things so he took one of these chickadees as his wife and he made the rest of them his maidservant, happy was these chickadees to serve the man o' heart coz they know he was a good man. Now these chickadees come from all across the land and they were all fair and they were all beautiful. Now in this land was many men who heard the good fortune of the man o' heart so some of these men offered their services to the man o' heart in order to gain favour with him so that they may take one if his maidservants in order to marry them and keep the faith and good practice of the man o' heart, this pleased the man o' heart coz it showed him that these men respected the teachings and the values that the man o' heart possessed. Now one of these men was a man o' war and his name was notorious throughout the land, and no one loved the man o' war coz he brings trouble to the land and wherever he go. Now when the man o' war heard of the good fortune of the man o' heart he became jealous coz his heart was deceitful and hardened nor was he kind or considerate, so the man o' war set out to challenge the man o' heart but the man o' war was not content in taking no maidservant for his bride oh no, he was only concerned with taking the bride of the man o' heart so he decides to war on the man o' heart and he plotted to kill him if he didn't give up the fairest of all the chickadees his wife.

Now the man o' heart was deeply troubled that another suitor had appeared to challenge his noble undertaking but he was not about to surrender his beautiful bride to a man of wicked deeds, so the man o' heart had to consider himself a plan to defeat the man o' war, so one day he call to the man o' war and he says to him if you can tell what the most beautiful and the most wonderful thing in the land is then I will freely give up my bride and be done with it but if you cannot then you must leave this land and never return. Now the man o' war stood there to think what the answer to the question would be, so he searched his mind for the answer but he could find none coz the man o' war was a lustful and envious and greedy and deceitfully hateful man and full of iniquity and the more he thought for the answer the less he could find it, and his impatience grew with anger and his impatience grew with rage to the point where he says to the man o' heart, if you don't tell me the answer to the question I will kill you, so the man o' heart says to the man o' war if I tell you that answer you must leave this land and never return, so the man o' war nodded his head in agreement and all the men and all the maidservants were there to witness it, so the man o' heart say to the man o' heart the answer to the question is love

Gad

Sensational Joe, now we must go immediately

Crowd

Hooray, we want Joseph, we want Joseph, we want Joseph,

Agent Rumsfold

No! No! This can't be, he's winning, a blasted 1st year, surely not, he shouldn't be winning the crowd over like this, its unfavourable to Generation 6

Crowd

We want Joseph, we want Joseph, we want Joseph

Agent Rumsfold

Seth stop this madness at once, do something, put an end to this yelling and uproar

Compare

And not it is done, so choose well your champion, as the clock strikes midnight and once and for all we can welcome the mighty ministry of Benjamin the Aries or Gad the Sagittarian

Crowd

We want Gad, we want Gad, We want Gad, Gad makes us glad

Compare

Congratulations Gad it is you the generations serve in all honesty and may you continue to grow and prosper in the year of our lord 3000 A.D, Happy New Year everybody!

Crowd

Happy New Year, hip, hip, Hooray!

....

Just as Joseph is about to exit the stage, Gad ushers him behind the curtains.

Gad

Yes Joe marvellous, absolutely marvellous, now as I was supposing that now we have Mary's Digital number to rely on, and that coupled with your number, allows me to get a match or fix on your daughter, and so if your number which is 1.4.7 Dome UK, and Mary's number is 2.5.8 Dome France, well at first sight I thought it should or could be 369, but then I realised, that when you break it down to its equivalent or difference, well then I suppose that what we are left with is actually 1.1.1, and so if the Child has now been allocated am Angel Digital Chip number of 1.1.1, then I can locate her whereabouts and pinpoint her placement in the Dome, and so therefore, this fixture of the Houses must signify, that the Child is now Generation 9, and is to be found in the 3rd House of Zebulon the Libran in Dome Europe Spain.

....

Compare

Now we shall hear from the one and only Obadiah 144

Obadiah 144

When does hope require a leap of faith, when does faith require a deeper belief, when does belief require the truth, if all is uncertainty then hope, faith, belief and truth is all we have, my Brother and Brethren, my sister and sistren, I wish to share with you today a story but not a story of the present but a story of the past but it still reflects upon us and the Generations of today, it is the story of Mary and her Child

Crowd

Tell us, tell us, we beseech thee, we praise thee

Obadiah 144

These new developments will soon become the normal and acceptable way of all things, that I believe is to be made clear, so it is better to work in partnership and together as those who have gone before us did so, we must also set aside any disputes or disagreements that may bring about the downfall or collapse of the traditions of the 12 houses, accordingly Sethaniel Newton and Tork of Naphtali and Agent Rumsfold were not completely wrong to join together in order to pursue or conclude the future of the 12 Houses, but what was completely unacceptable was the way in which they went about their business, they should have consulted the other houses of their intention and actions, as I believe this to be unforgivable, so as it is not my will to jeopardise the union of the 12, I can only but remove them from office and they will no longer play any role or take part in any matters concerning the houses, the authorities will deal with them accordingly, Obadiah 144 has spoken, so let it be a recorded document and testimony to all here tonight as we join in a universal prayer

Just then Angel Ruen approached the stage and stood to one side of Obadiah 144, as he begun to pray perhaps for the last time over the unsuspecting crowd, who had assembled themselves in bowing their heads graciously.

Prayer

Freedom beckons in the form of primal expressions, if only to overcome our mindful sufferings, and so therefore, we must go out of this world or otherwise remain confined in our solitary spaces forever shouting our and professing our obscenities of disappointment and dissatisfaction and discontentment at the top of our voices, if only to release the vile and the vulgar words of distaste, if only to once again reclaim the balance and order of our becoming once again, composed and dignified in the presences of our nature, as I fear above all else, that this could be our last days, and so it is at this time that we should stop waiting for a savior to save us, and to learn to accept and embrace our universal commonality as we go through each stage in these phases of life, Hear this forever after whose number is 7, holy recognizes the same and your world is now done, your thoughts have become one, in birth as of seven, show us today regular support because we are sorry and unfulfilled as those who are unfulfilled will turn against love, lead us away from enticement and guide us away from trouble, this is your world and your authority, and the recognition is yours eternally

And then for a moment after everything fell silent, until gradually everyone began yelling and screaming impulsively with such harsh and hardened expressions of ferocity within their voices, sounding and venting out their feelings with such an intensity of raw emotions using phrases of brutal and offensive and abusive language, wildly being shouted, as it hauntedly resounded throughout the air, and could be heard increasingly growing into ghastly fits of hysterics, that echoed loudly throughout Stereotypical, as this empowering and absurd reaction had served to release all their pent up aggression until finally their voices had

by now, turned into an elated feeling of uncontrollable laughter, after which Obadiah 144 had conducted the prayer, he was approached by Angel Ruen, who has been watching and observing all the events of proceedings as they had unfolded, and so now in being cautiously discrete, Obadiah 144 and Gad and Joseph, who anxiously stood behind the curtain in their readiness to disclose all the relevant details that the Angel Ruen had been waiting for.

Joe

Is this the Angel

Obadiah 144

Yes, this is the Angel

Joe

So what happens now?

Obadiah 144

You tell him what you know

Gad

Will she be harmed Angel?

Angel Ruen

No

Gad

Very well then you must go to Dome Europe Spain, for she is to be found in the 3rd House of the Ninth Generation, her number is 1.1.1

Angel Ruen

Very well then

....

Now when Angel Ruen had been made aware of the whereabouts of the Child of Mary Hampden and Joseph Blake within the Dome of the Domain and the Dominions, he felt an instant urge to act in such a way so as to fulfil an important part of the unspoken and unwritten contract between the Heavens and the Earth, as it was upon exiting stereotypical and leaving the Dome UK, that by now he was heading towards Dome Europe Spain in a bid to locate and retrieve the Child, and yet time was the master, but time could also be a disaster, for it was personally known to Angel Ruen, that soon the inhabitants of the Dome, were soon to be no more, and so he would have deliberate upon considering in saving this Child of nature, and to bring her into that part which is at the heart of Heaven, which is Nejeru, if only to preserve and to protect her humanity, and so it was that he set off in order to fulfil such a bargaining, for the true reason of this reckoning itself, which was the judgement that had been passed upon Angel Ruen in order for him to find and to seek out his own redemption, as Angel Ruen also knew that life and death were both intertwined and tied together like an exceptional and inseparable cord in that with him already being a subject of death, was knowledgeable enough to know that this would not be

the end of it, as he soon begun to realise that this Child, should not be subject to death as he had once been, especially if the living spirit were soon to reclaim the once pronounced Earth.

..........................……………………………………………......................................

Christina Scott and Joseph Blake eventually meet up again at the end of the proceedings and New Year's Celebrations.

Joe

Hey Chris, where you been?

Chris

I saw the whole thing, I can't believe it, was that really you?

Joe

I guess so

Chris

So what happens now?

Joe

I really don't know and I really don't care but one thing that I can say is that I'm glad it's' all over, oh yeah Chris, I figured out how to access the digital angel override, your original number was 217 and your present number is 126, I think Seth and Rumsfold have been playing you for a stooge all along

Chris

So I wasn't Generation 6

Joe

No you're not, your Generation 1, here take this chip it contains the blueprint for a digital override, see you around Chris

Chris

Thanks Joe

....

For even unto the celestial heavens and along the celestial equator, did they cover the whole of the entire Dome like a blanket of infinite light casting the purest glow that lit up across the breadth of that which once was the natural and purely organic and simplest of a living and breathing and fruitful planet, which was by now, being made ready for a divine transformation.

And so it was that the Angels of the celestial abode and those also of Empyreans had descended upon the Dome in their many forms and gathered up all of that which was the substance of the ethereal spirit of Mankind, and also of that with which was therein to be saved from the decays of this plagued and dying world, as the world was not to be destroyed but instead to be renewed in all its glory and splendour, but as it was, that there should be no living soul left upon its inhabitance to witness this renewal of creation.

For no one should be able to speak of it, or upon any account give any such reason, so as to be able to speak of it, for such an act of God, who in having no allies or partners, could only be caused to carry out this one singular motion of divinity, was that this living spirit would be caused to move once more over the earth, to reshape and to reform its' destiny, and to make it become ever more abundantly filled with life, in which could only be done in accordance and in the presences of none other, except than the Archangels, that is Gabriel and Michael and Raguel and Raphael and Remiel and Uriel and Zerachiel.

Authors Notes

It is of the utmost importance that we do not destroy any persons personal faith, no matter what or how profoundly they may aspire to be inspired to believe in something quite supernaturally or unfathomable, so please consider this and find it in your heart to know that faith is in the expression of living a life of piety and filled with a magnitude of love, as some of us put our faith in people as much as each other, as much as people put their faith in God or Angels or Spirits or Science, so I only say this, that with faith, it is only an attempt and a positive attitude that we are affirmed and just, in believing that the narratives that we are all aiming to pursue and fulfill and uncover, is to be accordingly just and right and true in our pursuits in this life, as such is the faith, that I have in all of you.

The Angel Babies Story for me, was very much written and inspired by many feelings of expression, that was buried very deeply inside of me, as it was through my own exchanges, and relationships, and journeying, and upon the discovery of both negative and positive experiences, that often challenged my own beliefs, and personal expectations of what I thought or felt was my own life's purpose, and reason for being and doing, and very much what any one of us would expect to be the result, or the outcome of their own personal life choices based upon the status quo of our own design or choosing.

The story within itself, very much maintains its own conception of intercession from one person to another, as we can only contain the comprehension of the things that we most relate too, and that which most commonly resembles and reflect our own emotions and experiences, by tying in with something tangible that either connects, or resonate at will deeply within us, as many of us have the ability and intuit nature, to grasp things not merely as they are presented to us, but how things can also unfold and manifest in us, that are sometimes far beyond our everyday imaginings, and that are also equally hard to grasp and somewhat difficult to comprehend and let alone explain.

As we often learn to see such challenges and difficulties as these, especially in young minds, that react in responsive ways and are also equally gifted, or equally find it in themselves in life changing circumstances, to deal with prevailing situations, that most of us would take for granted, and would naturally see as the average norm, as we are all somewhat uniquely adjusted to deal with the same prevailing situation very differently, or even more so to uniquely perceive it in very different ways.

As for the question of how we all independently learn to communicate through these various means of creative, or artistic, or spiritual measures, is also simply a way of communicating to God as in prayer, as well as with one another, as all aspects are one of the same creation, as to whether such forms of expression can personify, or act as an intermediate medium, or channel to God, or indeed from one person to another, is again very much dependent upon the nature of its composition and expression, and the root from which it extends, and so for us to believe that our forbearers, or indeed our ancestors have the ability to intercede for us in such spiritual terms upon this our journey through life, is very much to say, that it is through their life's experiences, that we have become equipped, and given a wealth, and a portion of their life's history, with which for us to make our own individual efforts and choices, for us to be sure and certain of the way, in which we shall eventually come to be.

When we take a leap of faith, it is often into the unknown, and it is often associated with, or stems from the result of our constant fate being applied and presented to us in the context of a fear or phobia, insomuch so, that we must somehow, or at least come face to face with, or deal with, or come to terms with these matters arising, that are usually our own personal concerns, or worries, or anxieties toward a balanced or foreseeable reality, which is often beyond our immediate control, in that we are attempting to define and deal with this systematic physical, and spiritual progression, in the hope and the faith that we can resolve these personal matters, so as to allow us to put the mind and the heart at ease and to rest.

As it is often through our rationalizing, and our affirmation, and our professing or living with our beliefs, that what we often call, or come to terms with through our acceptance, is that through faith, belief and worship in God, that such personal matters, can easily be addressed, and dealt with, so as to overcome when facing such difficult and challenging obstacles, as even when in response to a negative impact that can have a harmful effect upon our physical bodies and being, we also often rely upon this same faith in the physical terms of our living and well being to guide us, and especially where we are often engaged in rationalizing with this phenomena, in the context of our faith, hope and belief, which often requires and demands us to look upon the world in a completely different way, so that we can reach far beyond the rational expectations of our own reality, and perceive to look forward into that of our metaphysical world.

As it is through this metaphysical world of all irrationality, and chaos and confusion, that a leap of faith is required to pass through and beyond the unknown context of our rational and conscious reality, and thus so as far as we can see, to understand our consciousness, as we believe it should be, in that we are contained in every aspect of our faith, hope and belief, as we are often presented with more than just a rational imagination, of what lies beyond our eventful fate or worries and concerns, and so within the mind of dreams, we are presented with a super imagination, where extraordinary things exist and take effect much beyond our physical comprehension, although very much aligned to the interconnectedness within our emotions, that brings with it a super reality, where we can accept the tangibility of these dreams upon realizing them, so as to be found and understood, as when we are found to be waking up in our day to day reality and activity, but also in choosing not to deny or extinguish these dreams as mere dreams, but to accept, and to see them, or refer to them as signs.

As of when we see such tell tale signs, or such premonitions forgoing, or foreboding us in our fate, it is very much that these signs often impact the most upon that of our conscious minds, as they are very much presented to us in an informative and abstract way, very much like a picture puzzle that we are busily attempting to piece together and work out, and very much in the way that we are attempting to put the heart and the mind at ease and to rest, so as to secure peace of mind in order to find and establish and maintain inner peace, as such signs as these, are often the ones that I am referring too, and can often and easily be presented to us in many ways, but to be sure and certain, if they are Godly or Divining messages upon intuition and translation, very much depends and largely relies upon us as individuals, as to what we are naturally engaged in and pursuing, in the same hope and light of the context, of this experience of such a Godly nature.

As such experiences are crucial and key, as to how we deal with any or all relationships, especially when we are developing a relationship within the Godly aspects of our lives, as more often than not, when we use such phrases and metaphors as, 'Going through a Door' or 'Crossing a Bridge, it is simply by saying such statements as these, or putting things in this way or context, that we decidedly know and acknowledge that a big change is about to occur, and develop or happen to us, and so we in ourselves are becoming equipped and prepared to deal with such changes, as they shall determine what shall be the eventual outcome of our fate, as there may already have been so many foretelling signs, much before the final impact or infinite sign is presented to us, insomuch so, that it may have already been subtly presented to us, much before the true perspective or picture of our reality has come to fruition and presented to us as a whole.

The whole being, is that which pieces itself together, with all the necessary facets and aspects of our Human Nature, Personality, Mannerisms and Characteristics and Traits, as all in all, it presents to us a vision, which sets us apart from one another, but also equally ties us all together in the event and act of completing our picture and journey through life, and it is through these instincts that we all naturally possess, and is all that is inextricably woven into the metaphysical fabric and the spiritual aspects of the heart and mind, and of those that are channeled along the lines of the minds meridians, and the intricate channels that give way to apprehensible intuitive mental awareness of signs and dreams, and or premonitions or visions, of how, or what we may choose to accept, or to objectively analyze, or to take note of and perceive in communication, or indeed how God may choose to communicate with or through us.

As it is in our realizing that within our personal fate and decisiveness, that we are calling upon, and facing a reality, that questions and presents itself to us all, as something that is profoundly spiritual and ambiguous, in relation to what we are all intrinsically held and bound by within our faith and beliefs, in that what we expect is about to unravel itself before us, as we begin to discover all that in which we are, as such is the expectation and the realization in our phobias and fears, that we may begin to readdress or even regress, or desist in such a course of action concerning these doubts and deliberations, so as not to offset or to promote any ideas that may bring about any personal demise, or disharmony, or disunity, that may trigger any negative aspectual forecasts or emotions within ourselves, as it is such a self fulfilling reality, that we are all in subjection too, in creating along and upon our own individual paths of merits and natural progression, that naturally such phenomena is presented and revealed to us as a whole, and is often profoundly real and yet maintains its simplicity, and is quite ordinarily so upon our realization of it, as if by mere chance that somehow deep down we already knew, that when we became aware of it, we somehow knew it to be so.

As it is these lessons in life, that are to be learnt from such self affirming challenges, so as to test our minds imagination and of course that which is at the very heart, of how we in our Human nature, can so easily push our abilities far beyond the boundaries, upon the premise of what is, or what is not possible, which brings to mind the verse and saying of the scripture and that is to say, that if anyone adds or takes away from this book, then so too shall their part be added or taken away, and yet if we continue further along this point, it also goes on to ask, who is worthy to remove this seal, so as to reveal the dream or the foreknowledge that we may all come to terms with our natural agreement and acceptance of it, as it is in knowing and accepting what shall befall us in our fate, as to what choice of action we must or can take, as such are the phobias and fears of trepidation that also gives way to the rise of hope, so that we may come face to face with destiny.

As with each new day comes a new beginning, and with each new beginning comes new hopes and new expectations, as there are also new obstacles and challenges to overcome, as such is the dawning of life, to present to us all, such necessary and redeemable qualities within the observations of our lives, for to have hope, is to look up toward the heavens, and to quietly and silently know, that within this observation, that the sky or indeed the heavens, are still upheld by the forces of nature, that govern from above albeit much to our amazement and expectations, and that life is ordinarily and justly so, as we in our appreciation cannot always see beyond that which is so perfectly bound and set in motion with us in this universe, as we simply learn to believe and accept that this is the way of our living and all things besides us, as we are within all that has become created and laid out before us.

And yet with this new day dawning, if not for us to simply wake up and to use our hopes, and our aspirations to ascend beyond the obvious point of creation, and to apply our spiritual nature and positive will of motivation toward it, and it toward us upon reflection, as in our overcoming and prevailing, within its and our own destiny and deliverance, as such is also our descent to take warmth and courage, and comfort and refuge, when we lay down to take rest and sleep beneath the Moon and the Stars above, is also to take strength and peace of mind, in the hope and the understanding that a new day beginning, and a new dawning shall be presented to us once again, as this is the way of the life that we have come to know it, within our own divine ability and acceptance of it.

As much as life is and can very much be a challenge, it also appears to state, that there is a thread of universal commonality running through the whole of creation no matter what we profess to live and abide by as human beings, as for me the basis of these requirements that extend from this commonality is food, shelter, clothing, companionship, and a sense of connection or clarity derived from self awareness, that is not to say that there is not much more for broad scope beyond this basic measure and requirement that puts us all on an equal footing with one another, no matter where we inhabit or dwell in the world.

And so what and where are we permitted upon this universal basis, to gravitate towards, or indeed to excel to, in order to fulfill our existential experiences and engage with our full potential, as many of us in our progression towards modernity, would indeed interpretate this kind of idea or philosophy, depending upon which part of the world we lived in or inhabited, as being very much viewed differently realized upon that same broad basis, which also brings me to ask, and to question, and to examine this brave new world within this context, or indeed as some would profess to say or mention, within this new world order, or new world system, as there is much to address and to consider for all concerned.

For once we have evolved and grown and matured away from our basic needs and requirements, it would also appear that many of us who have indeed excelled, or concluded in the context of a post-modernistic era of environment or society, to have almost achieved something, which is of a value, or at least on a par with something that is equally attributed, to that of a spiritual level of attainment, or indeed enlightenment, but when we address the cost of such achievement, we also begin to see that we are still somewhat grounded in our best efforts by this basic requirement, which is to achieve, acquire, and survive at will, and to endure, and to live, and to abide by such new discoveries of achievements.

As even in this progress and achievement of what we would wish, or presume to call a new world, how do we fairly address or balance, or differentiate between those of us who are yet to grasp the basis of this understanding that is required for us to excel, or indeed for us to fly, or indeed to reach the highest spiritual level of attainment of understanding, of being, doing, and knowing, as in realizing that indeed not many of us could have, or would have had the opportunity, or indeed the privilege, of exercising such expressions of freedom in our new found world.

As some of us are fundamentally held by the very conventions of what is required upon this, a basic level of our independence, maintenance, and survival, to regulate and maintain the simplicity of ourselves, and yet once we have experienced and entertained this new idea inside such a concept, our first response is how should we, or what should we do in order to engage with one another, to bring about its universality as a basic principle and as a must for all concerned, and how can it be any good for us, if indeed we all profoundly have separate agendas, or different ideals, as to what should, or could take precedence over the basic and fundamental needs to live out our lives, when food, and shelter, and clothing, and companionship, and a sense of self, or a clarity of awareness is needed at the very heart of what it is, to not only be, but remain humane.

As for the background, or indeed the backdrop, and the combining and dedicated efforts, that it has taken me as a writer to come to arrive at within this story of the Angel Babies, and of course the time that it has taken for me, to construct, and to collate the necessary, and if I may say worthy and worthwhile aspects, for this particular body of work to become written and completed within the trilogy of the Angel Babies, I would very much like just like to inform the readership, that upon exploration and construction of this body of work, that I myself as a person, have experienced several variables of conversions upon my spiritual and emotional being, upon the instruction and initiation of bringing the series of these books into the light.

For had I not been introduced into the many schools of thought and allied faiths of Christianity, Islam, Hare Krsna, Hindu, Buddhism, Dao and Shinto, that it may never have transpired or surmounted, or indeed would have been very much an arduous and challenging task, to find the right motivation for the narrative, very much needed and applied, with which to find and devise the relative inspiration, and ideas explored and written within the context and narrative of the characters and the storyline that I have presented to you as an author.
~ *Clive Alando Taylor*

Angelus Domini
A Tao.House Product /Angel Babies
DOME.X.3000.MMM NEW AGE.
INSPIRIT*ASPIRE*ESPRIT*INSPIRE
Valentine Fountain of Love Ministry
Info contact: **tao.house@live.co.uk**
Copyright: Clive Alando Taylor 2016

Printed in the United States
By Bookmasters